]

The Big Crescendo

"Jonathan Brown hits it out of the park with this debut novel, featuring Lou Crasher, a smart, funny, hardworking drummer with a flair for detective work. The snappy dialog, realistic Los Angeles setting and quirky, compelling cast of supporting characters add to the fun. Can't wait for the encore."

—Anne Hillerman,
New York Times bestselling author

"Music fans, this is your book! In Lou Crasher, a journeyman drummer turned accidental P.I., Jonathan Brown has created a complex character set on a collision course with a cast of dangerous characters in and around L.A.'s music scene. With the pace of a blast beat, Crasher rumbles with a music theft ring, seedy drug dealers, and select members of L.A.'s elite, all while falling for a beautiful woman he is determined to help. Twist after twist, a breakneck pace, and the quick wit of Lou Crasher will have you turning the pages into the night. A wonderful debut."

—Shawn Reilly Simmons,
author of the Red Carpet Catering mysteries

"*The Big Crescendo* is a sex, drugs and rock 'n' roll mystery, played out at a breakneck 180 beats per minute. Amateur P.I. Lou Crasher does his hero Jim Rockford proud in this slam-bang, action-packed thriller."

—Paul D. Marks,
Shamus Award-winning author

THE BIG
CRESCENDO

OTHER TITLES BY JONATHAN BROWN

The Lou Crasher Thrillers
The Big Crescendo
Don't Shoot the Drummer (*)

The Doug "Moose" McCrae Thrillers
Moose's Law

Other Titles

A Boxing Trainer's Journey:
A Novel Based on the Life of Angelo Dundee

(*) Coming Soon

JONATHAN BROWN

THE BIG CRESCENDO

A Lou Crasher Thriller

Down & Out Books
3959 Van Dyke Road, Suite 265
Lutz, FL 33558
DownAndOutBooks.com

The characters and events in this book are fictitious. Any similarity to real persons, living or dead, is coincidental and not intended by the author.

Edited by Elaine Ash
Cover design by JT Lindroos

ISBN: 1-64396-048-2
ISBN-13: 978-1-64396-048-7

For Sonia Lucia—L'amore della mia vita

CHAPTER 1

Dry mouth, bloodshot eyes, the purple haze of a mild hangover. Not so much from booze, it was more lack of sleep and loud music. A normal start to the day, in other words.

I was getting ready to head to work when Michael, my immediate boss, called to send me on an errand. I am a musician, a drummer, but to pay the bills I work for Michael at a place called the L.A. Practice Joint, which sits a stone's throw from Hollywood High School in West Hollywood. "The Joint" is a place where bands, mostly the rock and roll kind, come and rehearse for gigs, demo tape recordings and new CD releases. We also have the hobbyist type that comes down to drink beer, smoke pot and "Jam, dude."

Ninety percent of the bands that come through The Joint are seconds away from signing the big recording contract, or so they tell it. It is my job to let them into their rooms, take their money, keep the place clean, and flash them a phony smile when they inform me of their impending fame. We charge a low rate and they treat the place accordingly. When they've completed their jam session, I make sure that the pile of crumpled single dollar bills adds up, kick them out and let the next soon-to-be-famous group through the gate, easy as pie.

When Michael called early this morning it was to tell me to

1

run by his parents' house to pick up the business phone, a seven-hundred-dollar phone. Seldom does a minute go by that Michael does not remind me and the rest of the staff of the phone's price, although depending on his mood, the price varies.

"No problem," I told Mike, and with apartment number, buzz number, address, and parking situation locked down, I was on my way.

My boss's parents own the business. They are a sweet elderly couple who flop over at the Knickerbocker Apartments on Hollywood Boulevard. I eased my 1965 Mustang into a roomy spot in a three-minute loading zone outside their place. I didn't have to worry about the time limit as the building was empty and a pleading For Lease sign hung in the window. This was no doubt another location where the businesses gave it the old three-month college try before having to pack it in—a sign of the times.

After repeating my name twice into the speaker, I was buzzed in. I wouldn't have put money on the elevator's chances of getting to the twelfth floor but she managed. Eddie, the owner, was waiting for me in the hall outside his door.

"You must be Louis," he said in a powerful voice that belonged to a younger man.

"Yes, and you must be Mr. Eddie Carruthers," I replied, pressing his flesh.

"Come in, come in, we've heard good things about you."

"Well, I'm glad to hear that," I said, stepping into the warm room.

The apartment was pretty much what I expected. It was very clean, too hot and overrun with knickknacks. What really caught my attention amid all of the old ornaments was the oversized flat-screen television. It was three sizes too large for the room, but I didn't protest, as Eddie had the football game on. The Denver Broncos were battling it out with the Oakland Raiders. Oh, how I wanted to call in sick, put my feet up and watch these rivals go at it, but how one calls in sick from his boss's abode is a mystery to me. The bottle of genuine draft at Eddie's elbow and its golden delight within didn't make things any easier.

"Here, sit down a minute. So, my useless son left the phone here and now you had to come out of your way and meet his old coot of a dad and the old battle-ax of a mother. Ain't that right, Evie?" he called.

"You know I don't respond to that kind of talk, Edward," his wife called from the kitchen.

"What the heck are you doing in there while we've got the whiz kid out here?"

As if on cue, Evie entered the room with a tray of milk and cookies. Eddie jolted forward in his La-Z-Boy.

"Milk and cookies," he blurted. "Come on Ev, he's a man, for heaven's sake, not a boy."

"No, no that's fine. Mrs. Carruthers, milk and cookies are my favorite," I said, standing as I remembered my manners.

"Liar," Eddie mumbled with a grin.

Eddie couldn't remember the "darned" score, so I got to perch on an ottoman until the score flashed on the screen. During that time Evie tried to get acquainted with me, but Eddie continuously shushed her.

Minutes later I was in my ride, not ten blocks from work. I rolled to a stop at a red light where Cahuenga meets Hollywood. I watched the steady flow of traffic from my left as I waited for an opening. I ignored the few pedestrians passing in front of my car, which turned out to be a mistake. A tall pimply faced kid with a nose ring reached in through my open window and snatched the phone from my passenger seat. Seven hundred dollars flew out my window quicker than I could select my favorite cuss word. I was going to get it back, plain and simple.

I cranked my car hard to the right and pulled in behind a flatbed truck loaded with shopping carts. Sliding my old-school steering wheel club into the locked position, I hefted it and hit the ground running. Up until my early twenties I played football at the free safety position up in Canada. That was, let's say, a few years ago, but I still had wheels.

How long my cardio would hold out was the big question, as I put the three punks between seventeen and twenty years of age. I gained on these kids immediately and it was then that my heart filled with hope as I remembered that kids today are raised on video games, junk food and cheap marijuana. They didn't play countless hours of kick the can, manhunt, and red rover like my generation had. It seemed that as children we ran non-stop from morning until the street lights came on. Cardio be damned, I was going to nail these suckers!

They made a right at the first street they hit. Pushing as hard as they could, the motley trio moved down the sidewalk, pausing occasionally to check my progress and to pull up their baggy pants. When one kid with a shaved head and a Green Day T-shirt abandoned the posse and darted into the street, a woman in a BMW 3 series with shocking red hair was forced to lock her brakes up. The kid was lucky she hadn't been on a cell phone or he'd have been one with hood and pavement. She leaned on her horn, and the kid responded with his middle finger.

"Run him over next time," I shouted as I sprinted past.

The pimply faced kid still had the phone, so I kept up chase on the remaining two. If I appear to be a fool rushing into a fight, I promise that this was not entirely the case. I have a background which consists of a variety of sports. In this case, a moment no doubt destined to end in fisticuffs, my years of playing football were sure to help. I played that game up until my twenty-first birthday. One thing I took away from my coaches was that even if you play on a losing team, you've got to just drop your shoulders and run through a guy and never stop driving those legs. Being on a losing team tends to toughen one up some, as it's often the other guy running over you. Also, I used to go a few rounds with a crazy uncle of mine, but more on that later.

An alley opened up in front of them to their right. The pimply faced kid took it while his partner, unaware of the plan, overshot the drive and fell to one knee. I caught up to him as he tried to gain his feet and threw a firm elbow into the small of his back. I could hear a tooth chip as his face made contact with the pavement. He yelped like a wounded poodle and let me know how he felt about it in Spanish. It was one of the three Spanish curse words I knew.

It was getting close to mano-a-mano time. The kid with the phone looked back to check on his cronies. Shock registered in his eyes as he saw how close I was. He tried to accelerate but it was too late. I pulled up beside him and swung the club at his legs behind the knees. He screamed as he went down. The phone popped out of his hand and slid ten feet on the ground before coming to rest beside the wheel of a garbage dumpster. I was panting heavily from the chase.

My veins overflowed with adrenaline. I put a knee in his back and laid the club across his neck the way a snake handler would position a lethal cobra. As I was telling him what I thought of him with choice words, the Latino with the newly chipped tooth tackled me off of his buddy. I suppose it served me right for trying to play tough guy/street lecturer. I now lay a few feet from the phone still with my club in hand. The Latino was up first and kicking me in the ribs or wherever he could. I got off a lucky swing that caught him on the shin.

It was not a fatal blow, but it was enough to make him change his plan. He leapt on me and tried to wrestle the club away. He spit in my face. I spit back in his but was not satisfied in the least. If possible, I was going to kill this man. The pimply faced kid was on his feet now and yelling orders at his buddy while calling me a "dead nigger" every five seconds. I decided I'd kill him, too.

Pound for pound the stocky Latino was probably stronger than me, but I was far more passionate. I tend to get that way when my ass is about to be kicked. He drew back to head-butt me. He was in perfect position to break my nose. I tried to get the jump on him and threw my head first, and our heads met, well, head-on. His face was now surrounded by pretty little

5

stars. He rolled off me with a moan. The pimply faced kid stepped over his friend and started kicking at me. I rolled away as fast as my aching head would let me. At one point he landed a kick at the base of my spine that sent a shock wave of pain from my toes to my earlobes, ending on the tip of my tongue. If he kicked me again I didn't feel it.

Certain that I was about to pass out, I was about to make myself comfortable when a loud voice commanded me to "get up." Whether it was the pimply faced punk or my ancestors I know not, but next thing I knew I was upright with wobbly legs beneath me. As my head cleared I remember what my uncle used to say when we goofed around at boxing. *If something comes at you get out of the way, then return the favor with something twice as hard as he was going to hit you with.* Wordy, but I got the gist.

The Latino was up, too, and back in the game. His twisted mouth raised on one side, revealing a bloody, confident grin. He slowly took off his plaid shirt, exposing large biceps covered in nasty tattoos. By nasty I mean he was covered in ink about death, guillotines, Rottweilers, pit bulls and bloody knives. I would have liked to have attacked while he was overdramatizing the plaid removal, but I still needed time to recoup.

"Rather than spend all that time in the chair getting ink done you should have been in the gym learning how to fight," I said, stalling, hoping for my legs to stop shaking.

"Is that right?" he asked with a smirk. "Why don't you drop that club and fight me like a man, tough guy?"

"Keep your girlfriend out of it and maybe I'll consider it."

The pimply faced kid's face reddened. "You're a dead—"

"Nigger, I know," I interrupted. "You mentioned that already. Is that all you've got, you little bastard?" My legs were nearly back.

"Listen, bro," the Latino piped in. "Let's stop bullshitting and get it on."

"Why don't you take her home and you two get it on?" I said.

That was the last straw for the man in the tattoos.

He charged me straight on. I held my ground as if I were slow to react and at the last second swung the club down in an overhand swing as if I were splitting a cedar stump. The club connected perfectly with my attacker's collarbone. All three of us heard the bone snap. He went down on one knee with a grimace but didn't cry out. He was definitely a tougher hombre than me. He was, however, officially out of the game.

I walked over to the phone and bent to pick it up. The pimply faced kid summoned up his courage and made a play for me. Again, I feigned unawareness. At the last moment, I stepped aside, letting the kid's own momentum carry him into the side of the dumpster. As he used the edge of the can to hoist himself up I brought the club down hard on his right hand, breaking it in at least two places. He screamed and slumped into the fetal position. He looked up at me with tears in his eyes and threatened me one last time. I considered tossing him a two-dollar line like "Crime doesn't pay," but decided against it. With club and phone in hand I walked out of the alley and back to my ride, which had a bright yellow parking ticket on her windshield.

CHAPTER 2

The L.A. Practice Joint is a dump. And for the record, I don't write home about it. The low-pile blond rug is now almost charcoal gray, and the eggshell walls are scuffed and gouged from floor to ceiling. The battle scars are not entirely visible to our clientele, as each wall is blocked top to bottom with rental amplifiers, drums, speakers and so on. An old slab of three-quarter inch plywood sitting atop two short file cabinets serves as our desk. I'm the only employee of The Joint who keeps the clutter on top of the desk somewhat organized.

I eased into the old office chair and put my own weary dogs up on the desk. I sat and stared at the phone, which slumbered happily as she charged despite the new scuff mark from the pavement. I let my mind digest the recent episode. My mother would have killed me had she known what I did. The same would go for my old man, though he would have better understood my actions. I suppose men can dig why other men do dumb things in the name of pride or bravado. I could just hear it. My father would argue with my mother that I acted on principle and my mother would have pointed out that it is interesting how often principle has to do with money or material things. Not a chance I would mention this ordeal to them during our next Sunday night call. The phone's ring startled me even though I was looking right at it.

"L.A. Practice Joint." Business voice.

"Yeah, uh, hey. Do you guys have rehearsal time over there…like available time, dude?"

"Yeah man, when did you want to jam?"

"Next Monday. No, Thursday. Yeah, no, Monday."

"So, Monday the tenth then?"

"No, dude, Monday as in tomorrow, dude, like man-ya-na, man." He giggled the oh-so-familiar pot-smoker's giggle.

"Tomorrow isn't next Monday, tomorrow is tomorrow, pal." I reached for my Tylenol.

"You're wrong, dude, you're so wrong. If today is Sunday and tomorrow is Monday then tomorrow is the next Monday we're going to have or encounter or whatever so I'm right, dude."

"Okay, smart guy, then Monday the third?" I said with a sigh.

"Hey, hey, hey I can hear the condescension in your voice, dude. Don't think I can't. 'Sides, the customer's always right, dude."

After playing musical days with the client for another five minutes it turned out that he was calling the wrong rehearsal studio. I enjoyed twenty minutes of peace until the office door opened slowly, the doorknob fitting into the hole in the wall behind it. Filling the doorway was a six-foot-two-inch blond transvestite in a pink tutu. The giant stubbed out her half-smoked cigarette under one of her four-inch stiletto heels. She leaned over the plywood and fed me Audrey Hepburn eyes.

"I'm here for the Pippy Longstocking audition. You see Pippy is smart. Pippy is sassy. Pippy is coy and oh, definitely sexy. And that's me. I'm going to be Pippy, the lead singer."

"Well yippee for Pippy. Let me check the book."

"Um, hello, you haven't said a thing about my look. Let me break it down for you, sugar. The tutu is from Aardvark, a secondhand store on Vine. The shoes were my mother's, may she rest in peace. The body is what Pilates can do for a girl with gumption, and the hair tie…" She paused to flip the wig. "Saks."

"Saks Fifth Avenue?"

"Oh no, sweetie I'm talking Saks Fashion Outlet. I don't go near those bitches on Rodeo, honey. Thank you, but no... thank ...you! Now the stockings, my favorite little accessory, are from Benny's Bunker on Melrose." She gave me a slow three-sixty-degree turn. "So? Don't leave a good girl hanging. What do you think?"

"Well, I suppose you'll make about the best Pippy they've ever seen."

"Oh, you are too kind." She put her index finger to her bottom lip. "Say, do you...?"

"I have a girlfriend," I lied.

"Figures. So where do you want me?"

"Studio B. You're the first one here so I'll just let you into the room." I walked her down to the studio through a perfume cloud thick enough for three women and let her in. I then turned on the P.A. system. "Good luck with the audition, big guy. I mean big...little girl."

I made my way back to the office and cracked myself a soda. Pippy's band was the only one scheduled for the next three hours, which gave me plenty of time to relax, barring more intelligent phone calls. Sleep snuck up on me unannounced. The smell of a sweet perfume, not Pippy's this time, brought me out of it.

I opened my eyes to see one of the most beautiful African-American women that I'd ever seen standing in front of me. But who was I kidding? She was the most beautiful woman I'd ever seen, period. Her dark ringlets cascaded over her slender shoulders like a gentle waterfall. Her eyes were a sharper green than mine, and much prettier. When she smiled they nearly disappeared into tiny little slits. Perfect teeth beamed through slightly parted sensuous lips that danced up to her dimpled cheeks. This was pure insanity. She had the kind of face that I wanted to see more of. It was also a face that made fashion photographers cancel the makeup artist before a photo shoot. Into their cell phones they chuckle, "She doesn't need any darn makeup. Take the day off."

There she stood, more beautiful than Nefertiti. Her tank top exposed tight abs and toned arms. A tiny lime green cell phone poked out of the pocket of her nice-fitting faded Levi's. She laughed as I stood and knocked my Pepsi into the garbage, which naturally hadn't been emptied, so the drink bounced off the debris, hit the floor and soaked into the dirty rug. Her laugh, which was another part of her I could get used to, rang out. It was like an intro to a Chopin piece played upon a finely-tuned Steinway.

"I'm sorry. I didn't mean to laugh. I'm Angela," she said, offering a hand.

"It's okay, really. I'm Louis or Lou, whatever you like...better. Welcome to the palatial Practice Joint. L.A.'s hottest..."

She raised one of her perfectly sculpted eyebrows at me.

"Okay, well then, welcome to a joint with totally reasonable rates."

"May I?" She motioned to the seat across from me.

"Of course, yeah, stay as long as you like." I sat without looking and nearly missed my chair. She grinned but held the laugh back. Bless her heart. We sat looking at each other. What I thought was a moment between us was merely a moron forgetting what his job was. If she hadn't cleared her throat I'd have kept staring until Christmas.

"Oh right. So, are you interested in jamming here? I mean is that why you're here? Of course it is."

"Why don't you tell me what your rates are?"

"Rates, rates are good." Somehow I managed to rattle them off without bumbling them up. Amazing, seeing as there were two whole different rates. She wanted a tour, so I gave her the best tour I could, elaborating, embellishing and elongating at every possible turn like a true businessman. And boy, did I want to make this sale. In fact, this was the first time I ever looked at this job as a sales job.

We have six rehearsal rooms at the Joint. By the fourth room

I'd already dropped my keys twice, banged my head on a speaker, sneezed, stuttered over the cancellation policy, segment of the spiel and turned on a sound system before checking the volume which caused the P.A. to scream like fifty tea kettles in our ears. I'd have had a better chance with Angela if I'd given the tour drunk on whiskey in pink boxer shorts. Who knows, maybe the court jester type would be her thing. The fifth room was the Pippy Longstocking auditions. This would be a great opportunity to take the idiot light off of me and shine it on the giant Pippy contestant. At the end of one of their songs I knocked once and we entered.

"Sorry to interrupt, fellas, I just wanted to give Angela here a quick look at our largest room."

"Angela?" the transvestite asked.

Angela replied, "George? Get out of here is that you?"

"Yeah, well, actually, it's Pippy now. Right guys?"

The three other band members nodded with grins on their faces. The audition was over. They had found their Pippy in George. Apparently, George and Angela went way back. They hugged and laughed, and when Angela introduced us, George mentioned that he'd already met the delicious chocolate gent from the front office. Angela smiled at me as if I'd just been let in on an inside joke. The pleasantries zipped around the room for another five minutes before we made our exit.

"So what do you think of George?" she beamed.

"Pippy can sing, and this chocolate gent is proud of him."

She put her hand over her mouth and giggled. They said their goodbyes and *I'll call yous* and we moved to our final room. With a six-month-old paint job and a ten-month-old carpet, room number six was our cleanest room. It also had the best P.A. system.

"...You mean I didn't tell you the story of this system? Allow me to introduce to you the system that once belonged to J.Lo. That's right. The story goes like this. J.Lo had this system in her Miami Beach home where she wrote, 'Jenny from the Block.'

When she was about to go on tour one of her dancers sprained his baby toe and claimed that the P.A. system was the wrong color according to feng shui. J.Lo agreed and that's when I got the call and passed the word onto my boss who picked it up for a song...no pun intended.

"J.Lo didn't like the color?" she asked.

"Yup, kooky, huh?"

"It's black, Louis."

I shrugged my shoulders. "So, what do you think?" I asked.

"Tightest little piece of bullshit I've heard this year."

"I've got to fix that story. At what point did you know I was, you know, fabricating?"

"Actually, the part when you opened your mouth was where you lost me."

She shook her head with the kind of grin on her face that women get when they've decided in their minds to go on at least one date with you, though they'd never vocalize it. We trod back to the office to wrap up. The Joint became a go for Angela. I could barely contain myself. She paid for a month's worth of rehearsals up front, cash. I'd never seen this type of business during my short stay at The Joint. The boss would do cartwheels, I was sure.

"Is there a problem?" she asked.

"No, I just...well, no, this is great news," I said. I wasn't sure where to put the money as there wasn't a chance in hell I was going to let her see the pathetic 1940's shoebox we use as our cash box. I decided to leave the money on the desk and just write out the receipt, which was also embarrassing, as my boss bought the cheapest receipt books that Sav-On carried. To add to this mess, we'd run out of them. I could only hope that she'd say "never mind" as I searched for what I knew I wouldn't find.

"Umm, you know what?" she said. Great, I was saved. "I think I'll go ahead and pay for two months right now."

"Wonderful," I said, "more money." I counted it and resumed my search, accidentally pinching my finger in the filing cabinet.

Being fleet on my feet I amended my curse word to 'Free Society.' This Angela woman had knocked my compass off its hinges, jerked the rug out from under me and set my inner pinball machine on tilt in under an hour.

CHAPTER 3

I wouldn't dare be so bold as to say that Angela liked me, but I was fairly sure I hadn't turned her off completely. Until. The transaction complete, she left with a smile. I was basking in her lingering perfume when I began doodling absentmindedly. My artistry became focused as I attempted to draw symmetrically perfect hearts with mine and Angela's names within. Silly, I know, but who'd see? Getting both sides of the heart even proved more difficult than I thought. Then her perfume grew stronger in my nostrils and there was the sound of a throat clearing. I dropped my pen and moved my horrified eyes slowly upward. She was back.

"Sorry to interrupt your, um, work. I just forgot my keys," she said reaching down to pick up a set of keys that lay not two inches from my artwork. I was so far gone that I hadn't noticed them. I hadn't felt like a little school boy since the days when I was a little school boy and even then, I thought I was a teenager. As quickly as this nightmare began it ended, and once again I heard her tiny footfalls moving down the hall. Depression set in.

Angela's band ended up booking three practices a week. Our rendezvous carried on much the same way as our first meeting: Angela the flawless damsel never in distress, and Lou the ever-bumbling buffoon. I was nearly as smooth as an intoxicated three-fingered, ten-pin bowler. The night of her first rehearsal, Angela came in wearing faded jeans and an oversized Dodgers jersey. The smell of roses, or maybe jasmine surrounded her as she politely asked that I fix the mic stand in her room.

"It just seems to be stuck. I don't know if you have another one or if you want to try to adjust the one in the room."

"Let's have a look. I'm sure it's nothing a little elbow grease can't fix." I got up from the desk and came around, trying to appear larger than I am. I said hello to some of the band members as I entered. The stand was stuck with the mic at waist height.

"As you can see it's too low. Do you think you can get it up?"

"Almost every time," I responded, soaking with wit. A few of the guys chuckled. I loosened the clasp with minimal effort but hoisted the mic with a little too much zeal. The mic collided with the underside of my chin at close to sixty miles an hour. The boys more than chuckled this time. At least Angela had a sympathetic look on her face when she laughed.

The next rehearsal was not much better. I simply had to have another glimpse of her fine figure in her black jeans and cashmere sweater. It was an old-school look, but she made it work. Having upped my workout program to three times per week, I decided rolling up the sleeves of my plain white T-shirt was a necessity. I crept into the rehearsal room to empty the garbage can. I jerked the bag out of the can with exaggerated ease, making sure her view of my biceps was not obstructed. The arm held, but even with minimal contents within, the bag did not. All I needed was the red clown nose. I made a note to thank my boss for the no-name garbage bags.

CHAPTER 4

My old gal, the 1965 Mustang, got me over the hill and into north Hollywood all on her own. It was as if somebody else turned my steering wheel and worked the pedals for me. It's like that sometimes when you meet someone new. Angela was the only thing on my mind. I was picturing us way too far into the future and it didn't bother me one bit. I knew I had it bad, but I loved it.

Once home I had to push my electronic garage door opener eleven times before the ton of rust reluctantly opened.

"Someday it's going to be me and you, pal," I threatened.

This open threat took me back to an old memory. When I was about nine years old I was up in my bedroom raising all kinds of hell. I was making such a racket that my mother came bursting into my room ready to break up what she thought was a fight between myself and some friend of mine.

"Boy, who are you yelling at like that?"

"This stupid Gameboy doesn't work. And it doesn't work cause it's a stupid son of a..."

"Don't you curse boy, not in this house. Not anywhere. Now why are you hollering at an inanimate object?"

"It's not inanimate, it's stupid. And now it's personal."

My mother spent half the day laughing at me after that one.

Now, I rode the elevator alone up to my apartment. When I got into my place I tested a theory. I took the battery out of my garage remote and swapped it with the one in my television remote. The television came on, but it wouldn't change channels no matter what angle I pointed it at the tube. I shook my head. All those years ago when I was upset with the "stupid" Gameboy, my mother came in and changed the batteries in the unit and had it working fine. Nearly three decades go by and I'm still the same dumb chump cursing inanimate objects.

I got up from my love seat, which has had so little loving since it has been in my possession that I actually just call it a seat. I called the voicemail number and put her on speaker. I got a pen and paper ready to write down my one-to-nine messages. The first message was Evie Carruthers.

"Louis, we heard about what happened after you left our place on Sunday. Sorry it's taken us so long to call. We meant to; the memory just isn't what it used to be. Anyway, are you okay? We hope you're all right. Next time just give them what they want. They're just, just bastards is all. Pardon my language, dear. Anyhow, you call us later and tell us how you are and…"

Her voice was interrupted by her husband Eddie. He was saying something in the background about how women are the only creatures on earth that can have conversations with answering machines. She called him an old grouch and hung up.

The next call was from the *L.A. Times*. Some cat was offering a great deal on subscriptions. They usually call every two weeks.

"…So if you're interested call us back and ask for Damien, that's me. And by the way your voice sounds very…um, warm. Bye-bye."

The next call was from Bobby.

"Lou! Listen, it's Bobby, you gotta back me up. I know I've said this before but this time is for real. It's my girl, Julie. I know that bi—I know she be cheatin' on me. I need you on this one, Lou. You gotta help."

Bob's one of those friends who always needs help, always

needs backup—essentially always needs. If he were a woman he'd be a drama queen. But Bob is not only painfully unaware of his high-maintenance personality, he's a colossal braggart. Yeah, he's that guy. I often wonder why we're friends.

I heated up some leftover spaghetti and downed two beers watching a Jimmy Kimmel rebroadcast. After doing the dishes I hit the sack. I fantasized that Angela and I were guests on Jimmy's show. We had a slamming funk band and played some really hot tune and then sat for the interview. With my luck Jimmy would direct all of his questions at Angela. My ringing phone brought me out of it. The number read unknown. Confident it wasn't a bill collector at that hour I answered.

"Hello."

"Lou? Sorry, Lou is that you?"

It was Eddie Carruthers, the late hour in his croaky voice.

"Yes, it's me, Eddie. Everything all right?"

"Sorry to bother you. Sorry to be up, actually. I think something might be going on at the shop."

I looked at my cell screen. "Almost four a.m. Should be quiet over there. What have ya got?"

"Well, the alarm was tripped but then immediately shut off."

"You check with Michael?"

"Yes, he's not picking up. Look, I hate to do this but would you mind swinging by and checking it out? I'll pay you for it."

Odd request but I needed the money.

"I don't mind at all, but did you call the alarm company?"

"I did and they said they didn't think it was a big deal. They also said that if I wanted a car to cruise by there'd be a fee."

"On top of what you already pay."

"Which I expressly pointed out to them."

"Which got you nowhere, and alas, it's cheaper to send the whiz kid down there," I teased.

"No flies on you, Louis. Would you mind?"

"No problem. And radio silence from Michael, huh?"

No response. I thought the call had been dropped.

"Eddie?"

"To be honest I'm not all that surprised I couldn't get him. I almost called you first anyway."

He sounded a little ashamed. Another awkward silence spread between us, so I broke it.

"I'm on my way. Do you want me to fill you in tomorrow, what with the hour and all?"

"Tonight if you don't mind. I won't sleep until I know what's going on, you understand."

"You got it, Big Eddie."

"Ha, ha, Big Eddie's what they called me in my gridiron days."

From the background Evie instructed me not to get him started. He called her an old bat, thanked me, then hung up.

The 101 Freeway was sparse enough for the ol' gal and me to hold pace at a smooth seventy-five mph. She can do ninety mph comfortably but I rarely push her there. We shot past the Highland exit and hit Cahuenga instead. This would allow me to circle around and into the driveway instead of making the left turn that nobody's fond of.

I made the hard right and nearly slammed into the high beams of something with size. I locked up the ol' gal's brakes. I was facing a truck for sure, the height of the halogens in my eyes proved it.

Neither vehicle moved. We were sandwiched between the two buildings at the mid-choke point. I could easily back into traffic, but this vehicle shouldn't have been at my place of business. It didn't belong to any of our staff. I tapped my horn once. The truck tapped back and inched forward.

Now I was pissed. I held my position. This was my turf. The truck eased forward. I looked out my window to see that it was a dually—meaning she had four huge back tires, two on either side so that the vehicle could haul a heavier payload than standard pickups. The truck had barely two inches on either side of her fenders. Her rumble was deep. I admired the truck but wanted to punch the driver in the face.

The machine inched all the way to my bumper and tapped my grill—actually, my hood. That was it. The big dog was the big dog. I put her in reverse and backed up slowly. Still, the truck gave me another bump.

Rage took over. I accelerated to the sidewalk but didn't enter the street. Instead, I slammed her in park and hefted my club.

"Get out!" I said.

The truck's engine revved. I could see three figures sitting across the bench seat. I walked to the passenger side and brought the club down, lopping off the side mirror. Someone in the cab called me a mother-effer. The driver punched and rammed my Mustang. It was my turn to use his phrase. My tires screeched, as the transmission was in park, brakes engaged. My front fender and hood popped a dent. Perhaps I hadn't thought my play through.

I ran back and jumped in her and gunned it into the street, and cranked the wheel. The truck caught air as it hit the street and pulled a hard right. I gave chase while trying to pull out my phone.

We tore up Highland to Hollywood. The light was red. Yes! I was going to go to town all over that truck without a care in the world that there were three dudes in it.

But the truck didn't so much as slow as it ran the light.

"Shit."

I came up hard to do the same thing but a 90's Toyota Camry came in hot from my left. I locked brakes up. Once she passed, I ran the light and immediately heard the joyous song of the law and saw the cherries behind me.

I pulled my ride to the right and considered getting out and running to the cop car but I knew better what with all of the shootings of the day occurring. My hands gripped the wheel at ten and two.

The cop's name was Taggs. I gave him everything I could

about the Practice Joint, Eddie Carruthers and my attempted citizen's arrest. He had one question.

"Did you get a plate?"

"Damn, there was no rear plate and in the front, well, we were nose to nose, so no."

"Interesting story, Mr. Crasher."

"Before you write me up can you accompany me to my place of business? I've got a bad feeling and here's why—the truck had gear in the box, and my place of business has gear and..." I paused. "We're closed and the alarm was tripped earlier."

"That's a lot of 'ands,' Mr. Crasher."

"Checking out a potential robbery has got to be more interesting than writing me a ticket, right?"

It aactually looked as though his brain-wheels were turning.

"Look, you'll probably get the call once I call 911 after you let me go, seeing as you're in the vicinity. So how about escort me over there, and if it's all clear, you write me a ticket and go on your way? If not, you're the first cop, sorry, *officer* on the scene. Hell, you might even make detective outta this," I said flashing a thousand-dollar smile.

His wheels continued turning. Sadly, they didn't turn in my favor. He finished writing me up and handed over the ticket.

"Ok, Mr. Citizen's Arrest, you've got me curious. I'll follow you over. Go easy on the accelerator," he said. "Unless you want another one of those." He grinned, pointing at my ticket.

Officer Taggs followed me into the tight lot. I nearly drove over our black iron security door, which was no longer attached to its hinges at the doorframe. We'd been hit, and I'd been grill-to-grill with the thieves.

Taggs insisted on entering first. I brought the hall lights up and we crept in. He announced he was LAPD and moved in. We went room to room, turning on lights as we entered. It was fairly obvious the crooks had split, which was the only reason he let me go in with him.

My heart sank once we entered room E, Angela's room. The locker she rented had the lock busted. The contents were gone, all of it. Taggs spoke into his shoulder mic and let dispatch know of our situation.

Although it looked like a smash and grab, the thieves found enough time to trash the room. There was graffiti on the walls and floor. The garbage can was tipped over but there was no debris because I'd emptied it at the end of my shift. Still, the thieves felt the need to spray-paint the F-word on it in red paint. They had some kind of carpet-cutter that allowed them to slice the carpet up. Someone even got up on a chair and pulled down a handful of ceiling tiles. After taking this in, we looked into Angela's storage locker. Her lock, still in the locked position, dangled loosely from the latch.

"A lot of good that lock did, Mr. Crasher."

"Do you mind if I make a call?" I asked, holding up my cell phone.

"Go'head."

I left the room and went to the office. As far as I could tell, it was undisturbed. I considered calling Eddie but reconsidered due to the time. It was time to find my boss.

"Hello?"

"Michael, there you are, it's Lou."

"Lou? What the hell?"

"I know it's late, or early, rather, but you need to get down to the shop. We've been robbed. I'm down here with a cop right now."

I imagined him throwing legs over the side of the bed and fumbling for his thick- lensed glasses on the nightstand as he peppered me with the standard questions one asks when woken from a deep sleep. I patiently repeated myself and told him I'd call Angela and tell her the bad news.

"I'm going to call my dad and then be right there."

"He did want an update, but I'd let him sleep. It was pretty late when he called me. What's another couple hours?" I said. "But it's your call."

"He called *you?*"

"He couldn't raise you, so he called me. Just get down here, Boss."

"Right," he hung up.

I went back out to check on Taggs. He wasn't in the studio. I found him in his cruiser working his on-board laptop.

"I called the boss. He's on his way. Do you mind if I make another call? I've got to inform the client from room E that her gear is in the wind."

He waved me off with a hand gesture as if shooing a fly.

Back at the office desk I put my feet up and checked the client book for Angela's number. I wasn't looking forward to waking her with bad news one bit, but it was all part of the job, I supposed.

There was gentle sleep in her voice, "Hello?"

"I'm so sorry to wake you, Angela. It's Lou Crasher from the Practice Joint."

"Uh-huh, it's five in the morning—why are you calling so early?"

At that moment, Michael, Officer Taggs and a cop I hadn't met came in.

"Hold on Angela—"

"Did you see the security door Lou? Did you see what they did? That door cost me close to twelve hundred installed. Man, I'm so sick of Hollywood."

Michael had tears in his eyes. I held up my hand, stopping him like a crossing guard.

"Angela?"

"Yeah, I'm here."

I gave her the CliffNotes version.

"Oh no! I'm on my way down."

Officer Taggs introduced cop number two as officer Rollins. He was bigger than Taggs and had a head the shape of a large block of ice. His eyes were small and close together and had a perpetual squint even though the windowless room was dimly lit.

We nodded to one another but we didn't shake. Mike explained that I had worked the day before and closed. Officer Rollins planted his squintys on me and let Taggs handle the questions.

"Mr. Crasher, did you see anyone hanging around that looked like they shouldn't? You know, like they were trying to scope the place?"

"There was the usual couple o' three Latino dudes that hang out on the sidewalk, but they're always there. They're harmless as far as I can tell."

He was unable to keep his career cop's suspicion out of his eyes. "Any prank or threatening calls?"

"Just one stoner confused about the days of the week," I chuckled but nobody else found the humor. Officer Taggs stood motionless with pen poised, waiting for something useful.

"Any bands here that you think capable of something like this?"

"If there was a riot and a music store window was smashed, sure there are a few guys in here that would step in and lift something. But rip that door off and rush this place? Nobody I can think of."

"You seem certain of that." Taggs shifted his weight to his opposite foot. Either his feet hurt or he was getting bored. I'm no master of body language.

"I'm just guessing like the next guy."

"What next guy?" He was staring hard now. He seemed harder all around since Rollins showed on the scene. *Cop machismo no doubt.*

I returned his hard stare, slightly confused by my own "next guy" statement. I could tell Taggs didn't like me. Blockhead Squinty Eyes' frown told me he shared the sentiment.

With a sigh, Taggs folded over his notebook and put his pen

away. He told us that they'd do what they could, but it was a long shot. Consider the valuables gone, in other words. They left us sitting there in silence. Mike finally excused himself and reached for his phone.

Footfalls came down the hall. We turned and waited as if for a celebrity to emerge for a curtain call. Angela came through the door in black boots, blue jeans and a loose, cream colored long-sleeve cotton number. She wore no makeup and didn't need it. She was the only beautiful thing in the office and, as men, we puffed out chests and straightened postures as if we each might have a sliver of a chance with her.

I got up, came around the desk and gave her a hug, which she accepted. She hung on a second longer than I expected. I could have stayed there all night.

"Everyone, this is Angela. Hers was the locker that got popped in E."

A chorus of "ohs" and "tough breaks" filled the tiny office.

Angela and I walked into room E and looked at the damage.

"They must have used a crowbar or tire iron to pry that lock latch off. It would be easier than trying to crack it open."

She stared in pain, as if hoping the stuff would just materialize on its own.

"What happens now, Louis?" Angela's voice cracked a little.

"I suppose I'll help the boss clean up and then chill until my shift later."

"No, I mean what about my stuff? You guys must have some sort of theft insurance, right?"

"Absolutely," I assured her while having no clue whether we did or not.

"That's something, I guess."

The cops' cruisers could be heard firing up in the parking lot. When we got back to the office my boss was red-faced, talking into the phone.

"...No, you listen to me, man. My parents have been with your company for twenty-five years, so don't tell me that because my payment is past due you're not covering me... What?... Oh really? You'll be hearing from our lawyer! What's that? Never mind what my lawyer's name is smart-ass, you'll know soon enough!"

His attempted confident tone told us—as well as the person on the other end of the phone—that there was no lawyer. Mike nearly slammed the phone down until he remembered it was a cell phone. Not good for slamming. It also would've defeated the purpose of my previous knuckle skinning.

"Those A-holes at my insurance company don't want to cover me."

He sat down hard with a curse. *So much for my earlier assurance to Angela.*

"Tough break, Boss. Do you want me to start cleaning this crap up?"

"No, this fight isn't over yet. Dad's coming over and we're going to photograph the place. If they do eventually cover us, we'll need to show damages."

He pulled off his baseball cap and ran his fingers through gray-specked hair, then replaced the cap. "This fight isn't over yet, as I said, Lou. Take five—a long five. I'll call you in a few days."

At the end of the hall I grabbed Angela gently by the shoulders.

"He's right, Angela, this is not over. If I know Michael's dad, who actually owns this joint, he's got a policy Michael may not even know about—he's old-school thorough like that."

She nodded her head up and down and her weak smile became stronger. I smiled back.

"Where are you parked, Angela?"

"On the street, around the corner. Why?"

"Let me walk you to your car."

The morning smog cloud hadn't burned off yet. On days like these tourists often assume that the day is going to remain overcast or even rain. But by noon the sun would be out and tearing through L.A.'s thin ozone.

Angela had a BMW 3 series. I was impressed with the shape

she kept the car in. She'd upgraded the rims but didn't go overboard with the flash, which in my opinion ruins most cars' aesthetic.

"So you dig German engineering, eh?" I threw that out to lighten the mood.

"Eh? That's Canadian isn't it?"

"Yes. I'm originally from Vancouver. I came here to be a rock star," I paused and glanced at my watch. "It should happen any day now if you're looking for a coattail to ride."

Her nose crinkled into a short giggle.

"Incidentally, 'Eh' may be Canadian but 'huh?' is American."

"Well I don't use 'huh.'"

She crossed arms, pretending to be mad. I took a step closer to show I was no pushover.

"And you will never hear me say 'eh' again…lady."

"Come on, let's go get breakfast, Scarface. I'll drop you at your car later."

She punched me lightly on the shoulder. I walked around the car, trying not to grin too hard.

As embarrassed as I was to admit it, I confessed that I was craving IHOP pancakes.

"If you had to pick," I said, "—say, on a desert island, what would it be: IHOP or Denny's?"

"I love my Grand Slam breakfast, but it would have to be IHOP."

"Right on! You're the best."

"The best? How would you know about that?" she inquired with serious eyes.

"Well, I don't mean anything. I mean the IHOP. I wasn't being sexual. Not that you said or even thought—"

"Relax, brother, I'm just playing."

"Girl, you should be an actress. You scared the-you-know-what out of me. Give me a minute to catch my breath."

"Now who's the actor? Catch your breath, my foot."

We drove along Fountain Avenue as far as we could before

28

easing down to Santa Monica Boulevard where the IHOP stood proudly. A friendly Latino man with a twenty-mile-wide grin valet-parked the Beamer. Angela gave the hostess the name of Louis-Louis but pronounced it "Louie, Louie" like the song by The Kingsmen.

"Now you're trying to be cute," I said.

"Don't you think I'm cute? I thought that little heart you were drawing was, I don't know, because you thought I was cute."

"I categorically deny drawing any such thing," I pouted. "It was simply a cross section of a leaf magnified one hundred times. I have a thing for biology."

"Biology, I'd have thought you had a thing for women. Oh, well."

"Vocalist and a comedian, are we?"

I tried not to look at her as she smiled at me.

"And yes, you are cute, I suppose."

Just then the hostess called my new name. "Louis-Louis. Party of two? Louis-Louis?"

Angela nearly fell over laughing when I raised my hand like a student, acknowledging that this ridiculous name was mine. An elderly couple waiting for their table looked at me with pity in their eyes.

I ordered the Passport Breakfast, which has been one of the top three breakfasts in North America for decades. I may not be able to show any valid documentation, but I truly believe it in my heart. The Passport has pancakes, sausage, bacon and eggs the way you want 'em. It is paradisiacal, to say the least. Angela ordered the Rooty Tooty Fresh N Fruity, no doubt unaware that she looked as cute as a mouse's ear when she said it. It was basically the same as the Passport, only you got to choose a fruity topping for the pancakes. She went with blueberries.

"Good choice. You know, blueberry pie is my favorite type of pie."

"Do they actually have blueberries in Canada? I thought it'd be too cold."

"I can hardly contain the laughter over here, Angela, please stop."

"I like that you call me Angela and not Ang or Angie."

"I'm glad you like."

"What about you? Do you like Louis or do you prefer Lou?"

She sat low in her chair with her elbows on the table, leaning forward so her chin hovered two inches above her clasped hands. It gave the effect that she was hanging on my every word. What a doll.

"I prefer Lou, except when you say 'Louis.'"

"A charmer. Momma told me to watch out for boys like you."

"Boys?" I reply with raised eyebrows.

"Pardon me, men like you."

"That's better."

She rolled her eyes and shook her head. We smiled at each other over our coffee mugs.

"Again, I want to say how sorry I am about your equipment, Angela."

"It's all right. It's not your fault. Besides, I've had a brainstorm."

"Oh yeah?" The fog of guilt that surrounded me began to lift.

"Oh yeah, I have a proposition for you."

"Proposition is a good word."

"Why don't you find my gear for me?"

"Excuse me?"

"Hear me out. You have connections; bands that come in, other practice studios and so on. Why not use those resources and track down our stuff?"

"Angela, there are trained professionals that do that jazz. I'm just a drum-kit drummer. I can't even play the bongos."

"Huh?"

"You said huh?" I smiled.

"Whatever, but what do the bongos have to do with...?"

"Nothing, I'm just saying I wouldn't know how to find..."

"I have money. Well, I can get money from my producer,

and he can go to the label and get you some money. We'd hire you as a detective...dude."

It was dangerous how well she could sell.

"No offense, brother, but I know Mike isn't paying you what he should be paying a brother."

"I won't argue with you there."

"Play P.I. for a few days until you go back to work. What do you say?"

"I say that with those eyes of yours you could crack any witness on any witness stand any day, talk any jumper down from a building, and smile a rich man out of his money."

"Slow your roll. So you'll do it. How much scratch do you think you'll need?"

"Jim Rockford used to charge two hundred a day plus expenses. I love that you say 'scratch.' I do too, by the way."

"Do you mean *The Rockford Files*? Aren't you a little young for that reference? My older brothers used to watch that show."

"I've always been a fan of things late '60s and '70s. I may have been born in the wrong era." I smiled.

"Retro brother, huh? Now having said that you ain't getting no two hundred a day."

"Plus expenses," I added.

"Sorry, Bub. Bring it on down."

"One twenty a day flat...and I'm firm on that."

"Done," she said. We shook across the table.

"Cool, but one last thing: you did say 'huh,' earlier. What's up with that?"

CHAPTER 5

I rolled out of bed around nine-thirty a.m. On the nightstand was an equipment list with serial numbers that Angela scribbled before we bid adieu last night. I'd asked for any distinguishing features: stickers, dents scratches, marijuana butts, or roaches in any hidden compartments. She had more information than the average musician.

After a short jog followed by push-ups and sit-ups, I hit the shower. I tend to exercise more nowadays seeing as I'm no longer playing any organized sports.

The first stop was the city of Woodland Hills. A healthy amount of studio musicians and rising-star actors flop in this area. The neighborhoods are quiet and clean, and many homes sit on properties sized so a gardener can make a decent buck. The musicians' union operated the first space I went to, which meant the place was state of the art and the prices were high. The guy running the counter was obviously an English literature major, maybe even an unpublished writer frustrated by his station.

"Good morning. The name's Lou Crasher."

"And?"

"And I'm in pursuit of some stolen musical equipment. Perhaps you could—"

"I haven't the slightest notion as to what you are accustomed, young man, but I assure you that at this establishment we do not entertain artists who would even consider possessing stolen equipment."

I wouldn't put money on it but that sure sounded like a run-on sentence to me. Best not to bring it up at this juncture, was my thinking. I did, however, need to relate to this scholar on his level, or at least close to it. I cleared my throat.

"Dear sir, I am accustomed to the known fact that some artists are not unlike a few bad apples in that they come by their instruments, or gear, if you will, ah, ah, dishonestly. I mean, this is Los Angeles after all, man."

Take that, I thought. Either I had him on the ropes or he was appalled at my verbiage, for he said nothing. I plunged on.

"Am I to understand that your claim is that you know the origin of each, every, and all pieces of equipment that cross that threshold and into this burgh?"

My tongue now had a headache.

"Precisely, and this is no 'burgh,' as you put it."

I needed another way in. It was time to take myself down a notch. I needed to relinquish power, as talk-show therapists say—kissing ass, in other words.

"Look, I'm sorry, man. I didn't mean you or this fine establishment any disrespect. It's just the pressure of the job. You see, I work in a place like this in Hollywood. Of course, my place is non-union and quite dumpy compared to all of this." I spread my arms and looked around wide-eyed as a child might upon entering the gates of Disneyland.

"What did you say your name was again?"

"I haven't mentioned it but if you must know it is Nigel, Nigel Brixton."

"Nigel you and I aren't so far apart. We're in the rehearsal space trenches, man. They don't appreciate what we do. We're underpaid and often waylaid. Hell, listen to your elocution, not to mention diction! You should be on the lecture circuit doing book signings, the whole nine yards...my good man."

"My good man" meticulously removed his wire-rimmed spectacles. He tucked them gingerly in his breast pocket. From the depths of his pomposity rose a minute smile. I'd got him.

"A thankless job it can be. I most certainly will not argue that," he sighed. "Be thankful you don't work with some of this lot. One would expect decent behavior from symphony musicians and respected jazz practitioners. Such is not the case. 'What do you mean you're out of Yamaha music stands?' 'Why don't you carry violin strings?' 'The Steinway piano in room two has a sharp E key.'"

He raised his voice. "As if you could tell, you Berklee College of Music bastard!"

He paused, deflated, and then cursed and pounded the table with a bony fist. He'd feel that later. With an apology and another sigh, he walked to the back, dragging his feet as he went. When he re-emerged, a leather-bound logbook was under his arm. We found only one band that had rented a storage locker that would jive with my search. He led me to it, popped the lock and let me have a look. One amplifier was the right make but the serial numbers were way off. I thanked him and gave him a copy of my list, as well as a contact number. He spoke to my back as I was leaving.

"This business of ours can ruin a man. If you have dreams, young man, I suggest you follow them."

I promised that I would, and bee-lined to the exit as his eyes were filling with water. I'm not particularly good at the grown men and tears gig.

"Young man," he said as I had one foot out the door.

"Yes, Nigel."

"Please, a moment if you will," he said, gesturing me back with a long bony finger. As I strode back to the counter he pulled the specs from his breast pocket and cleaned the lenses with his pocket square.

"There was one bloke not long ago that I was forced to not only reprimand but banish, as well." He seemed proud of the fact that he'd seen action—or what I'm sure he thought was action.

"This brute was scheduled to rehearse in room number three but was caught exiting room four. An honest mistake, he claimed. That was until the vocalist from room five screamed bloody murder that her priceless Sennheiser NKS 500 microphone went missing. We deduced that this man was the culprit. But, when we searched his person," he paused. Nothing."

The clerk's eyes were expectant, so I whistled low as if impressed. But I needed more.

"So what happened next?"

"I tossed the brute and told him never to return." And with that Nigel folded his arms, prideful.

"But with all due respect, you said he didn't have the mic," I said.

"A simple sleight of hand, my good man. If you'd seen his beady little eyes, you'd have seen his guilt clear as Christmas."

"Wow," I said unable to muster anything clever. "Do you remember the, ah, brute's name?"

"Yes, it was Dave something. Abernathy or Abigail something like that."

I thanked him and we shook hands. At the door I thought of something else.

"Just curious, what makes the Sennheiser NK etcetera a big deal?"

"She's got a top-notch transmitter and a beautiful, slick alloy nickel finish," He paused, seeing that I wasn't catching the drift.

"And you can't purchase her for under three thousand dollars, Mister Crasher."

"Aah."

"Aah indeed, Mister Crasher. Good day."

Prior to firing up my ride, I opened the notes section in my phone and entered what I'd learned from my pal Nigel. As the drumming detective, my next stop was the Valley Jam Spot, which sat on the Sherman Oaks/Van Nuys border.

As I walked through the door I was slapped in the face by such a strong marijuana smell that I was forced to grab the counter for stability. A sturdy gent in a black and blue plaid hooded sweatshirt with cut-off sleeves sat at the helm. Dirty, stubbed feet in five-year-old Birkenstocks sat atop a messy knotty pine desk. It appeared that in the 1990s he'd taken a dull knife and made his favorite jeans into cut-off shorts. Long black greasy hair splayed over his heavy shoulders. His mouth and left eye were smiling. Good pot. I couldn't tell what the right eye was doing, as it had a navy-blue pirate patch over it. The smile remained fixed, so I threw words first.

"Excuse me, man. The name's Lou and I work down in Hollywood at the—"

But that's as far as I got before he burst with laughter and exhaled a huge cloud of smoke.

"Sorry dude, I'm not laughing at you, or the fact you live in Hollywood."

"Work in Hollywood."

"Right, sorry, it's just this killer weed, man. Whoooo!"

"I can dig it."

"You like?" he asked, offering me a pull on a joint he had hidden beneath the desk.

"In my youth I like. Anyway, the reason I'm here is we had a robbery at the Practice Joint and I'm stuck with running down some of this gear."

"It sucks to be you, Mack. That's a job for someone like..." He looked at the ceiling and waved the joint around in a circle searching for an example. I got tired of waiting.

"Columbo?"

"Who? No, Nathan Fillion, dude who plays Castle on the show of the same name."

I'd totally baffled him. He knew what to do with the joint, however. He took another pull. I handed him my list of gear. He lifted the patch off his eye to read the list. After far too much scrutiny he handed the list back to me.

"I got nuthin'. But I will tell you this though Mack; I heard about what happened to you guys down there. At least I think I did…" Both Birkenstocks now moved in unison like windshield wipers.

"No, that was Greg's in Long Beach. Oh yeah, it was—no, that was Vinny's up in Bakersfield. I'm sorry, Mack, the memory's shot. All that bad weed in the early 2000s. I got good shit now though. Are you sure you won't…"

"Retired," I responded. "And what's with calling me Mack every three seconds?"

"Isn't that your name? You said it was." He shrugged it off. "Suit yourself on the non-smokeage. Say…there is this, though. If I were looking for stolen stuff I'd look at Dave Abbott."

That had to be the name Nigel was trying to recall.

"Is that the guy who used to sing for Napoleon's Fallopian Opus?"

"That's the same dude, dude. D'ya ever hear about what he really does to make dough? He steals and fences the very kind of jazz you're talking about."

"No kidding?"

"Hey, on hemp's honor. If I lie, stick a reefer in my eye."

"Nice little poem." I said, keeping it friendly.

"Thanks," he said proudly, then suffered a cough attack so fierce he was forced to throw both Birkenstock-clad feet to the floor and pound the center of his chest with a chubby fist.

"Whoa, can't say what the hell that was all about."

He was struggling to catch his breath but still managed to re-fire up his joint and take a deep pull.

"I just remembered another thing about Abbott. We got high cause I do that sometimes."

Really?

"And I had some really good shit, so we were like dusted, dude. Anyway, we're talking bands and shit, then we talk gear and all of a sudden this guy's bragging about stuff."

"What kind of stuff?" I asked, leaning on the desk.

The big stoner raised his eye patch and lowered his voice to a whisper. "He says he can get me any brand of guitar within twenty-four hours. Any brand. You believe that shit, bro?"

I gave the big stoner the same low whistle I'd given Nigel Brixton. The eye patch stayed on top of his head for the remaining five minutes I stuck around, listening to him attempt to recall more Dave Abbott stories.

Finally, I told him that I didn't think Abbott would add up to much and thanked him for his time. This was not entirely true, but I didn't want him remembering me if asked. The fact of the matter was I knew of Dave Abbott's reputation quite well. He's every musician's Public Enemy Number One. Even if only half of the rumors are true, he's still responsible for ripping off thousands of dollars' worth of gear over the years. Why he has never been caught is a mystery. Some say he's connected. This is why I blew off Mr. Birkenstocks; I don't need any connected heat on my case.

I walked back to the parking lot, pulling lungfuls of fresh air. Back in 2007, Abbott's band was on their way up. They'd gotten signed to a new record label with heavy financial backers. They had limos, radio play, wine, women and lousy songs, in my opinion. Just before going on tour the band started fighting and called it a day. The record label wanted their invested money from the band and put the squeeze on Abbott. It is believed that Dave began selling off gear to pay his debt. Running out of his own supply, he began ripping off other bands' gear and selling it.

The kicker is that the record label had two other main artists that simply weren't putting up the numbers. Investors got nervous and pulled out. The label threw in the towel. All bets were off and nobody came collecting. Abbott was a free man. But greed does what greed does, and Abbott became accustomed to the stolen property bullion. He kept making our tough lives tougher.

My memory clicked through snippets of info. Back at the Mustang, my phone buzzed. I didn't recognize the number.

Normally I'd leave it to voicemail, but figured a P.I. on a case takes all calls—it's what Jim Rockford would do.

"Hello?"

"Mr. Crasher, Nigel Brixton here. I remember the bloke's name we spoke of earlier. It was Abbott not Abernathy, Dave Abbott."

"Thanks Nigel, you're a man among men."

"Not at all. But promise me if he turns out to be the guilty party you'll kick him square in the bollix for me, will you please?"

"Consider it done, Nigel."

He clicked off. Dave Abbott was now my prime suspect and would have been from the moment I took this case, if I were a real private investigator.

CHAPTER 6

I had the feeling a drummer gets when he's laid down a monster track in the studio. I could feel in my bones that Dave Abbott knocked over my workplace. He was on my radar and I was going to bring him down.

Musicians and crime fighters all over Southern California would thank me and lie about knowing me. The old gal was on automatic pilot all the way home as I was busy grinning like an idiot through traffic. Even my cantankerous garage door couldn't pry the smile from my mug. As I waited patiently for the door to rise, a shape flashed across my rear-view mirror. Kids. Always up to something, or appearing that way at least. I pulled into my usual spot next to my neighbor's 1966 Cougar XR7. I'd only seen her once when the owner had pulled the car cover off for me to see. She was *cherry*, as they say. Windows up and steering wheel club fixed, I stepped out of the ol' gal. A strong perfume hit my nostrils. When I got out an attractive Asian woman in her mid-twenties stood by the trunk of my car.

"Whoa, you startled me. Hi, I'm Lou."

She held a pink purse shaped like an old army trunk only it was so small that when she held it in both hands only four fingers and two thumbs fit on the strap. Her pink sweater was ribbed and hadn't complained once so far about the torso it was housing...

And that made two of us. I couldn't make the brand of the jeans, but I think the company should've offered her a modeling contract.

"I'm Hi," she said, "and I don't mean stoned. It's short for Hyacinth." A petite hand left the trunk and shook like a much bigger hand. "I'm sorry that I startled you."

"Oh no, no it's fine. I'm fine," I said, giving her hand back.

"My car won't start. I wonder if you could help me."

"Your wish is my wish."

"Excuse me?"

"Never mind." I tell her. "Which way is it to your ride?" I ask.

Naturally, Angela is the only one for me, even if she doesn't know it yet, but the way Hyacinth clicked along in her little pumps, just-so, was really putting pressure on my loyalties. The beat-up 80s' Chevy Caprice Classic she claimed to own was a big motor for a petite girl. The vanity license plate read KICKAZZ, which was another oddity for such a cute waif. The beginning sound of a warning bell went off but was cut short A half-step before the car, a quarter stick of dynamite rocked my skull. The-day-after-a-concert ring blared in my ears. Someone sapped me again from behind like the true sap I was. I vaguely remember the pavement rushing quickly toward my face. Somewhere between the conscious and subconscious lay Lou Crasher, totally unconscious. Totally crashed.

A bump in the road woke me. I didn't have to be a real P.I. to know that I was in the trunk of the Chevy. At least it wasn't a Smart Car. I decided not to attempt picking the lock or tunneling through the back seat. Knowing one's limitations saves pride and prevents panic. I'd wait it out and see who my captors were and what their plan was. I could hear the muffled voices of three to four people mixed in with obnoxious punk rock music. The car rolled over some rough terrain, like pot holes or train tracks— briefly—then skidded to a stop. The music quit. Two doors opened. Two doors closed. Footsteps. No dialog, just the sound of dancing keys. I closed my eyes and the trunk opened. There wasn't much difference in light through my lids. Hands grabbed at me and I feigned grogginess so I could count numbers and hope for an opening.

"Come on, bitches, get him outta there."

"Shut up, Travis, we are. He's heavy, man."

"You wimps, I'd do it myself but this prick busted my hand. Okay, good, hold him steady. Hey there, asshole," he says to me.

It was the pimply faced kid from the alley. He slapped me with his good hand.

"Snap out of it, man. I want you to see what you got comin.'"

"Travis, is that your name?"

"That's right, asshole."

"How's the hand?"

He came in for a punch this time. Using the two guys holding my arms back as leverage, I kicked Travis square in the family jewels. He went down chirping like a budgie. The man on my left reefed so hard on my arm I thought my shoulder was going to pop. The other guy fed me a solid punch to the gut. I doubled over. A familiar pink trunk purse came rapidly into view and caught me on the nose. My eyes watered as my heart pounded angry blood into my veins.

This, in turn, fueled my adrenaline motor. I was categorically pissed. Pitching forward forced them to let go of my arms. I fell on Travis, my hands having no problem finding his throat. My grip tightened on his neck as though it were an orange I intended making into fresh-squeezed juice. His eyes popped open wide with terror. I began to chuckle as I tasted the blood from my bleeding nose. The trunk purse came in for another shot. I released one hand from Travis's throat and easily pried it from Hyacinth's hand. My plan was to drive the purse through Travis's face and out the back of his skull when his other two pals pulled me off of him. I rolled away from their kicks as best I could.

I caught a glimpse of Hyacinth helping Travis to his feet. He called to his boys, "Let's get the fuck outta here—I gotta ice my fucking nuts. You're dead, Crasher."

I took one more shot to the gut before the soccer players

heeded their master's call like dogs and ran to the car. I closed my eyes against the tire-spent gravel. Travis had just made a huge mistake: he left me alive.

CHAPTER 7

I felt like finding the coziest-looking rock I could lay my hands on, using it as a pillow and catching as close to forty winks as possible. Ah, but I decided against it. I had a home and all I had to do was get to it. I knew I was still in the San Fernando Valley because there are some things a guy just knows. Exactly where in the Valley was something a guy didn't know. I started to make tracks downhill toward the freeway lights. Once close enough to read the off-ramp sign my eagle eye told me I was in the city of Chatsworth—California's pornography capital, us what some people claim. True or not, this little tidbit wasn't going to help me any. Barring any freeway traffic, the old gal would have me home in fifteen minutes. She wasn't here, so that was out.

Although never a math whiz, I managed a quick count of all my fingers, toes and more precious body parts. The math added up. My watch was gone (all twenty-five dollars' worth of it), but to my surprise I still had my wallet and all its contents—including sixteen bucks. I was livin' with an apostrophe "n." This was now the smart money, and the smart money said for me to walk to the nearest gas station and have a taxi pull me out of this porno town.

Hopefully, the walk was no more than twenty minutes in length, as my weary bones would have me searching for the comfortable pillow rock if I tried to push it past minute twenty. Moving slightly faster than a snail in her teens, I'd been mobile nine minutes when a late-model Chevy Avalanche truck passed me from the rear then skidded to a halt thirty feet in front of me. Reverse lights piped up and the truck rolled slowly back to stop beside me.

"Lou? Is that you?"

"Mackerel! Are you ladies a sight for sore bones."

"What are you doing out here? And who tap-danced on your pretty face?"

"A couple o' punks who don't see things the way I do. Oh, and there was a woman with them, too."

"There usually is, Lou. Hop in."

"Kat, Tami, you guys are looking awesome as usual."

"Well, Lou, you've looked better."

"I'll be all right. So what about you two? I haven't received any notice about the grand opening of your gym, so I suppose it hasn't happened yet? Or did you forget about your favorite drummer?"

"To answer your question, no, we haven't had the grand opening yet. But let's forget about the gym for now and tell us what you're doing all beat to crap out here in the middle of nowhere?"

Kat is a gorgeous raven-haired Korean black belt. She's petite but can hit like a Mack truck. The hard look she gave made it clear that small talk was out of the question. Tami, her partner in crime—also a black belt—is black. She fed me the same serious look from the driver's seat. She, too, is a knockout, I might add.

And so I gave it to them, the semi-abridged version of my abduction. It felt odd talking about it—as though I were describing an event that happened to someone else.

"So you were knocked out in your garage and that means concussion," Tami said.

"Not my first."

"Either way we're taking you to emergency," Kat said.

"What? No way, I've been in worse scrapes, ladies."

"We can't be moved on this, Lou."

"Is that right? And do you ladies go to emergency every time your bell gets rung during sparring matches?"

The truck cab went silent. "I didn't think so. Now, if you'd be so kind as to drop me off at my North Hollywood Penthouse, I'd appreciate it."

"Fine," Kat said. "No hospital, but someone's got to keep an eye on you tonight. We didn't rescue you from the roadside just to wake up tomorrow and hear that you slipped into a coma all by your lonesome."

The cab became quiet again.

"We get off this freeway in three exits Lou, what's it going to be?" Tami asked.

I was outnumbered and definitely out-gunned. "I have an idea," I said, hauling out my phone. It survived the fight but had a dead battery.

"May I borrow one of your phones?"

Kat handed me her over-sized cell phone.

"This phone is bigger than you," I said, thanking her.

I dialed Angela's number. I'm not usually in the habit of re-membering clients' numbers but hers was locked like a drum track. Perhaps it had something to do with the fact I was head-over-it for her.

"Hello?"

"Angela, it's Lou Crasher from the Practice Joint."

"Oh, that Lou Crasher," she teased.

"I have an odd favor to ask."

"Ask."

Kat and Tami's ears were peeled back as far as they'd go. They hung on every word.

"I've been hard at it hunting for your gear and got some promising stuff. But at the end of the day, well, I got into a bit of a dust up with some morons."

"Dust up?"

"A fight. Anyway, my nurses are worried that I may have a

46

concussion and that I shouldn't be alone tonight."

Tami elbowed me in the shoulder for my 'nurses' comment.

"Would this brother be asking too much if he could crash on your couch tonight? Feel free to say no."

"Of course, Lou. Should I text my address to this number?"

"Yes, please do. And thanks so much. I owe you one. What city are you in, by the way?"

"Sherman Oaks."

I repeated it, making sure the ladies heard me. Tami nodded.

"Great, we should be fifteen minutes or so, and thanks so much."

Angela's door swung inward. "Oh my god, your poor face. Come in, come in."
I stepped in and she closed the door behind me. She gave me a gentle hug, careful not to injure, then led me down a short hall past a narrow mahogany entry table with a round ceramic bowl with keys in it. The bowl looked like it could star in a home-decorating show. She guided me into her living area and eased me into a plush beige sofa.

I twisted around and watched her walk past a marble-top island and into her kitchen.

"I'm going to make you some tea. How's your head? Want some Advil?" I wanted to let her play nurse for the next ten years. She was a genuine sweetheart.

"Might you put a little medicine in that tea?"

"No booze Crasher, this is serious," she said, topping up the kettle and plopping it down on a five-burner stainless steel stove. My ribs were too sore to maintain my twisted position, much as I enjoyed the view, so I turned toward her fifty-five-inch mounted television. She had the news on with the volume low. I checked out the reading material on her chunky wood coffee table.

There was a *Shape* magazine, a *Musician's Monthly* and a *Bon Appetit*. Angela came over and handed me two aspirin and a glass of water. After I knocked them down she sat beside me, took a damp cloth and gingerly went at my face. She was forced to get close. The combination of her sweet smell and perpetual expression of concern had me weak in the knees. It was a good thing we were sitting.

"So you said you were out there doing the gumshoe thing today, huh?"

"Which reminds me: I caught myself a pretty darn good lead, too. A guy—"

I stopped as we both heard a commotion coming from her TV; Angela turned and brought the sound up. We were looking at a group of people in panic mode, crowding around a woman on an EMT gurney. She was convulsing like Linda Blair in the original *Exorcist* movie.

The onlookers were all young girls in miniskirts.

"Looks like a bachelorette party went sideways," I said.

The girls were screaming and crying. The paramedics vainly attempted to push them back. The girl nearly flopped off the gurney. A newscaster's voice told us some new concoction of mystery coke had claimed its latest victims.

She put the rag down and said, "So you were saying something about looking for my stuff."

"There's a cat by the name—"

Her kettle screamed on the stove. "The tea!" she said, leaping off the couch.

She came back with a tray and what some might consider one of the cutest tea sets in America. We sipped our tea like an old couple. Could this be foreshadowing? *Steady Lou.* I thought back to Abbott and was about to open my mouth again when Angela's cell rang. The ringtone was "Superstition" by Stevie Wonder.

"That's my aunt, I need to take this, sorry." She grabbed her phone from the island.

"Aunt Lonnie, is everything okay? Yes...I see...uh-huh...no, I don't think anyone would steal your glasses...no, they're such nice people at the home...have you tried the drawer beside your bed...no, beside your bed...okay, I'll wait." Angela gave me a sad smile and mouthed "sorry."

"Not at all," I whispered.

"Yes, I'm here, Aunt Lonnie...oh good, I'm glad. Was there anything else? Did you eat today? Honest? Okay, you have a good night. I love you, too."

She sighed heavily and came back to the couch.

"My poor aunt. Early onset dementia."

"Sorry to hear that, doll. She found her glasses though?"

"Yeah, same place as always."

Our heads rested against the sofa back. With faces close we stared at each other. I thanked her again for taking me in. She propped herself up and smiled down at me. Her ringlets dropped forward, framing her face. I smiled back as she came in slowly and kissed me on the lips. It was slow at first, then our lips parted and our tongues met...and got to know each other.

We kept it up for who knows how long. I lost track of time, space, everything. For the record I was fully up to the task of taking our kiss to the next level—going the distance if need be—but a breathless Angela whispered "too soon" before getting up and making her couch into a bed for this battered drummer.

CHAPTER 8

I woke to the smell of bacon, eggs, toast and coffee—never mind the whole nine yards, this was the entire football field as far as I was concerned. It almost chased away the ache in my bruises. Almost. This Angela gal just got better and better, I was falling hard for her. As a journeyman drummer slugging it out on the L.A. music scene, I rarely got the opportunity to lock lips with a specimen as fine as Angela.

I grinned like a fool the entire ride from her place to mine. I grinned broader still after we engaged in lengthy kiss number two in her Beemer outside my apartment. As I stared at her disappearing back bumper, I realized the name "Dave Abbott" had never crossed my lips. No biggie. The real prize would come when I found the gear and returned it to Angela.

As I stepped from the elevator, a thickly built brother in a tight white T-shirt and blue jeans leaned against the wall outside my door.

"Jake, what are you doing here?"

He didn't answer, which is par for the course with Jake. We met accidentally a year and a half back. Jake was posing as a liquor store clerk for a friend. I happened in on the place during an armed robbery. I was able to help Jake, meaning the good guys won. Ever since, Jake has acted as though he owes me.

I let us in. Jake sat at my crappy kitchen table. He looked massive in my kitchen—an alcove so small a naval submarine cook would call it tiny. I yanked two beers from the fridge, popped tops and handed one to Jake. We took long pulls and set them down.

Jake gave me a short nod with a slight Clint Eastwood-style squint. I'd read his sign language long enough to know that he wanted to know about my bruised face. So, I laid out the entire symphony for him without missing a single movement.

We were two-thirds through our beers when I was done. Jake hadn't uttered a single word. He barely moved an inch, save for an occasional flexing of his jaw muscles or ripple of his thick cord-like veins crawling over his muscular forearms.

He declined a second beer and had only one question: "How do you want to handle this Travis guy?"

"I don't know if I want him handled exactly. I just need the guy off my back. I can't very well recover this gear if the idiot makes a play for me every five minutes."

"You haven't answered my question."

"I want to send a message. I want to put the fear into that punk. I want to catch him off guard at his crib when he's not backed up with his little entourage. Can you dig it?"

"That can be done."

"Seriously?"

"You mentioned his plate, KICKAZZ, that's how we find him."

"You can do that?"

He didn't answer. He just sat still as a statue chiseled from onyx.

"What exactly do you do for a living, Jake? You've never told me."

"Haven't I?"

And with that he got up and strode to my door.

"So, you're going to run that plate down then?"

That got me a nasty scowl.

"Cool, and thanks."

I followed him into the hall and spoke to his back, "I'm going to reach out to an old friend at The Percussion House, you know, in case you want to know what I'll be up to."

The exit door to the stairwell slowly closed behind him.

CHAPTER 9

I followed Jake's lead and declined my own offer of a second beer. I had a long hot shower, which eventually turned cold. I'd seen a fitness guru on TV talk about the healing powers of cold showers. Figured it couldn't hurt.

Normally I'd have made a sandwich for the road, but my belly was still full from the breakfast Angela had fed me.

I got dressed and headed down to my underground lot and checked it more thoroughly than a bloodhound on a manhunt. No way was I getting sapped twice. With the coast clear I fired up my ride.

On the 101 Freeway South down toward Hollywood, I was heading back to my alma mater. As nearly every make, model and year of vehicle barreled down the six lanes at seventy-five miles per hour, we looked like flying metal insects heading to different hives. As bumpers and grills narrowly missed one another, I wondered how many other cars ferried private eyes. Not that I was a bona fide P.I. or anything.

I took the Gower exit to Franklin and headed east. Ten minutes later I was at my destination.

The Percussion House is a small music school that romanced me down to Los Angeles in the first place. When I attended, the school held six hundred students, and counting. It was founded in 1995 by two local studio musicians. Sheila Moore, a talented backup singer and ghost lead vocalist, sang many a high part for metal singers in the late '90s. Her partner, and later husband, Joe Styles, played dozens of lead guitar solos for big-name cats on days when the big-name rocker couldn't cut the big-time solo for the record. Players like Joe and Sheila were paid handsomely for their silence, which is why few people knew of them, or believed musicians like them existed.

One June afternoon Joe and Sheila met and hit it off. Although vocalist and guitar player, they both shared a passion for percussion. Before either could play, sing or tap a note they were shacking up in Pasadena. They loved to stay up late, sit naked on the floor and play various Latin and African drums as a sort of rhythmic foreplay, if you will. Their favorite night was Saturday when they could play louder and longer with limited neighbor complaint. It was also the night they'd allow themselves to indulge in the pleasures of marijuana and red wine.

Next, out would come the big drop sheet, body paint and so on. A few years later they tied the knot and began hunting for just the right instructors for their school. With all of the ducks lined up, the school was born. All who attended knew of the weed, wine and drop-sheet ritual, as the instructors weren't shy about mentioning the nights in their lectures. They were going for a sort of New Age, early 1970s type of hippie atmosphere. After all, the best players played from the heart. *Rimshot Magazine* did a piece on the school, which was how I discovered it many years later. Drums in a free love, friendly environment—sign me up.

While going to The Percussion House I became tight with one of the receptionists. Her name was Stacy Krunch. I tumbled head over it for her, but she insisted that I was too young. I liked her for letting me down easy like that, what with her three puny years on me. Perhaps it was a maturity thing. I mean, I was all bug-eyed, buck-toothed and pigeon-toed when I stepped on L.A. soil those few short years ago. We kept in touch from time to time, but not like in the days when I was a student.

Lives get in the way. Stacy had umpteen million connections. She also ran a musician's referral service on the side and rumor had it she was kicking butt.

Her office door was open. She smiled as if she'd been expecting me.

"How's my milk chocolate-y Crispy Krunch?"

"Sweet Lou Crasher, as I live and as I breathe."

She came around her desk and gave me a big hug.

"How're ya doin', Stace?"

"Good, good. How're you doin'? You must be working 'cause you haven't called my service."

"Ah, but it's never enough."

"I hear that. So what's up?" she asked.

"Have you got a minute?"

"For you I have a minute and a half," she said, moving back behind the desk.

"Ooh baby. Here goes. I don't know if you know it or not, but I'm working at the L.A. Practice Space."

"I do now. I heard you guys got hit the other night though. How bad was it?"

"Not good. Question."

"Shoot."

"Who hit us?" I thought I might get lucky.

"What am I, a detective?"

"No, but I'm pretending to be one."

"Oh, Louis." Here it comes. "I hope there's money in it, as well as the woman you're chasing."

"Stacy Krunch, I'm shocked."

"So snap out of it. Who's the broad?"

I paused, busted. "You don't know her."

"Um-hm," she said.

"Let me get to it. What do you know about Dave Abbott?"

"He'd sell his mother if he hasn't already. And if you're hangin' with him, this conversation is over."

"Settle down. Nobody's hangin' with anybody. Girl, I can't

believe you'd think—"

"So believe it," she said. "What's the deal?"

"He's Suspect Numero Uno, so give me what you got."

And with a sigh she gave me Abbott's story—the abridged version.

"He had a bunch of projects on the go. He was a wheeler-dealer of musicians and equipment. He got his fifteen minutes with a group named Napoleon's Fallopian or whatever they were called. You know how he stiffed his band and all that?"

"Yeah."

"I don't like this guy, Lou. You be careful. If the walls start closing in, you call in the serve and protect fellas, ya hear?"

"Will do," I said saluting her.

"Let me see if I have an address for him. Here, he signed out some ACDC videos back in the day and gave his girl-friend's address. Write this down, Mr. Dick, I mean detective."

"You're hilarious."

"And I'll be here all week. Twenty fifty-five Digby Drive over in Silverlake. Don't ask the apartment number because it's a house. Now give me a hug and get out of here, pretty eyes, I've got work to do."

CHAPTER 10

Jake leaned against the driver door of his Dodge Challenger and watched the world go by. His ride had four-hundred-and-seventy horses under the hood. Jake never sped; never received a speeding ticket—ever. Still, he liked knowing he had the muscle under the lid should he need it. He watched as drivers and pedestrians moved to destinations they believed were more important than everybody else. The citizens in the biggest hurry, and of most import, seemed to be the ones heading into coffee shops. *Addicts*, Jake thought.

Jake pulled out his phone and scrolled through his contacts. When he found who he was looking for he opened the text window, typed: KICKAZZ, and hit Send. The number ten came back immediately. That meant he'd get back to Jake within ten minutes.

A homeless man sat cross-legged with his aging beagle outside a laundromat. He shook as though he had Parkinson's. Several people walked by, ignoring his empty collection hat.

Jake walked up to him and put five dollars into the hat.

"Thank you, sir, God bless," the man said, looking up. He was missing his left eye. A victim of the brutal streets, Jake thought.

The man shivered slightly once his good eye was on Jake. This was fear. Jake elicited this response at times. The beagle growled low in its chest.

"How are you holding up out here, young man?"

"Ha, I haven't been a young man for fifty years, son. But we get by, Rusty and me."

The beagle wagged its tail at hearing his name.

"Are you hungry?"

"I'm all right," he said. "But they make a hell of a burrito at the vehicle over there."

"So I've heard," Jake said, getting up and walking to the taco truck. He bought two burritos and gave them to the homeless man.

"God bless you, brother. What did you say your name was?"

"Jake. Yours?"

"Rusty, Rusty senior, that's Junior."

Jake stuck twenty more dollars in the hat. "Hang in there, Rusty."

Rusty Sr. thanked him. The beagle barked.

As Jake walked back to his car his phone vibrated. It was a text from his contact. Travis was Travis Jenkins and he lived at sixteen-sixteen Sycamore Drive, apartment three-o-four, in West Hollywood. Jake knew the street but not the sixteen-hundred block. He opened up "maps" on his phone and found it. Then he climbed into the Challenger and woke all four-hundred-and-seventy horses.

When I stepped out of the Percussion House my phone buzzed. It was Jake texting me the address to Travis Jenkins's. I called Jake back.

"Thanks for the heads-up Jake, I'll let you know how it plays out."

"I'm going in with you."

"No need, pal. My old man taught me to fight my own battles."

"You're not a hundred percent. Besides, he might have his

entourage, as you put it, with him."

He had good points. Even if he didn't, Jake wasn't someone to argue with.

"I'll be there in ten."

When I drove up, Jake was leaning against his badass ride, six cars down from Travis's Caprice Classic. My temperature rose as I walked by and looked at the trunk that previously housed me. I nodded to Jake. He didn't move a single taut muscle.

We went into the dusty multi-story building and rode the elevator in silence. My heart rate was pounding in my ears. I used to get the same feeling on the rides over at my unhinged Uncle Curtis's, especially on the days I knew we were to spar. But this was slightly different. I felt fear in those days. It wasn't fear making my mercury rise in this elevator; it was rage.

"Just relax," Jake said, as if he could sense my energy.

We walked past two doors before reaching three-o-four. The music of heavy metal band Pantera easily found its way through Travis's door. The pungent aroma of marijuana accompanied the band.

"Do we knock? Kick it in, what do you say, Jake?"

Jake grabbed the handle and leaned against the door, but not with much pressure. He then let go, rolled his neck around with a crack then rotated his shoulders back and around a few times. I knew not to interrupt. With legs slightly bent he grabbed the door handle again and leaned hard into the door. Even in jeans I could see his quad muscles grow. His neck and trapezius muscles appeared as though they'd rip through his skin.

The door gave. The molding and jam splintered but couldn't be heard over the loud music. We were in. I went first. We wouldn't have fit side by side in the short corridor. A tiny bathroom popped up on our left. I stepped in and cleared it quickly and rejoined Jake.

We emerged at a combo kitchen and small living area not too dissimilar from my own—built in the same era, no doubt. Travis's TV had at least ten inches in diameter on mine and on it was a porno movie with the sound off. The couch facing the screen put the back of his head to Jake and me.

We couldn't see his hands and didn't need to as his head and torso were gyrating in such a manner as to be expected when one watches such a movie alone. I gave Jake a disgusted look.

A small wicker basket on the kitchen floor contained dirty magazines. I picked up the whole thing and tossed it high over Travis's head. It landed square on the coffee table in front of him. The basket broke a tall glass marijuana bong in pieces, sending glass and bong water everywhere. Travis jumped up with a scream familiar to me. He scrambled to get his privates back into his jockeys as he spun toward us.

"What the fuck? You! And who's this asshole?" His hand shook as he killed the music with the remote. Jake moved to the bedroom and checked for occupants.

"Where the fuck is he going?"

"Turn off the video Travis," I said.

Jake returned, "Clear."

"My house, my video."

I took a step toward him. He killed the video.

"You assholes think you can just come in here and—"

"Stop talking. We just came by to say that whatever this little obsession is that you have with me is over. Capiche?"

"What the fuck does that mean?"

"It's Italian for—"

That's when Travis produced a knife from his couch cushion and wielded it in his functioning hand. He lunged at me with a straight stab. He was faster than I expected. I threw my hips back and avoided the strike. He came back with a side-slash. I repeated my move and received a slice to my shirt—too close for comfort. I was running out of real estate. I couldn't pull the same move a third time. I needed to end this.

His next attempt was an underhanded swing for my face. I snapped my head back, feeling the wind of the blade cruise by. I saw an opening and sent a short left jab, catching him on his pug nose. It didn't have the heat I'd desired, but still, it sent him back into his rickety dining table. I adopted a fighting stance and eased forward. If he thought he saw murder in my eyes he was dead on.

Something went off in his eyes—a plan. He wound up like a baseball pitcher and threw the knife at me with everything his scrawny little arm could muster. I dove to the ground, knowing I'd never be fast enough.

Jake must have seen the play in Travis's mind before he did. That is what fighting is, after all—knowing what the other guy is going to do and neutralizing it. Jake grabbed a skateboard that was leaning against a dilapidated bucket chair and launched it end-over-end.

It collided with the blade in flight, carrying both objects into a six-foot-high steel bookshelf with glass shelves. The shelves shattered to the floor with a loud crash. I was back to my feet, fighting stance returned.

Travis charged with a high-pitched scream. He couldn't get to me fast enough. I was going to extinguish the punk's pilot light for good. Jake must have sensed my rage and didn't want me to catch a murder beef.

He headed Travis off and grabbed him one-handed by the throat. Travis looked as though he'd run into an invisible brick wall. He gurgled, squinted his eyes shut and grabbed Jake's hand in both of his own. It was no use. Jake's grip was a human woodworker's vice, applying maximum PSI.

I slid up to him. "What's your obsession with me, asshole?" I asked.

"No, nobody kicks my ass you ass, ass—hole."

"You referring to our brawl in the alley? You're a child Travis, get over it, unless you want to see us again."

Jake applied more pressure causing Travis' face to redden. His eyes ballooned wide with terror before losing focus.

Jake let him drop to the floor. Travis was out cold. I'd never seen a one-handed choke before—didn't know it existed.

A voice with irritation in it came from down the hall.

"Travis? Travis, it's Mr. Gremlin, the landlord. What the hell is going on in there?"

I moved down the hall and greeted a balding man in his sixties at the broken door.

"Afternoon, Mr. Gremlin—sorry about the noise. I promise we'll keep it down."

"Who are you?

"Not to worry, Mr. Gremlin, I'm a contractor, name's Jimmy Beam of Beam Construction. Travis and I are heading out for materials, then we're coming back to fix the door."

And where's Travis?"

"He's getting changed; we're heading out."

The landlord wasn't buying it. He eyed me suspiciously and tried to look over my shoulder. I blocked his view and began easing the door closed.

"It's been a pleasure meeting you Mr. Gremlin," I said closing the door with a car salesman's smile.

"But—"

He told me through the door that Travis was on notice. Footsteps stomped away.

"Jimmy Beam? As in Jim Beam the whiskey? Really, Lou?" Jake asked.

"It just came to mind. Is he still out?" I motioned to Travis. Jake didn't need to answer. Travis was snoring.

"Do you think the message has been sent, Jake? Do you think this will do it?"

He didn't answer. I looked at the busted bong, shattered bookcase, dining table on the brink of collapse, demolished entry door and the big bruise forming on the slumbering greasy bastard's neck.

"Yeah, I suppose we're done here," I said. "Let's blow."

CHAPTER 11

When we were outside, I thanked Jake and told him that I was going to head over to the domicile of Dave Abbott's girlfriend. She went by the name Candy Striper. Jake said nothing.

"What are you up to now?"

"Do I seem like the share-my-itinerary type?"

He eased into his ride, fired her up and rumbled down Travis's street. I shook my head and thought back to the night we'd met.

It was nearly two years ago. I'd only just completed music school when I had a gig forty-five minutes north of L.A. After the show, I pulled into Bart's Liquor for some freeway munchies, just next to a black Kia something-or-other. A slim Latina woman about nineteen sat looking nervous in the passenger seat. I nodded to her for no other reason than courtesy. Her nervous eyes left the storefront for under a second to meet mine before swinging back to the front door.

Two large garbage cans propped the front doors open. As I was stepping past them the horn of the Kia honked rapidly, four times. "Shit!" I said as a man with a gun in his gloved hand moved his weapon off of the counterman's face to level it at me. Horror stories came flooding into my brain. I raised my hands automatically. "Down on the floor, asshole," the gunman shouted at me.

The counterman, a thickly built brother who looked far too calm, shook his head at me to ignore the command. I don't know why, but I began to feel calm when I saw the counterman's eyes. In fact, this dude seemed so cool that I felt he was in control of the situation.

"I said down on the floor, brutha. And you, fill up this fucking bag, counter boy."

The opposing counterman yelled for me to get out. He didn't have to tell me twice. A shot went off. I sprinted to the old gal and fired her up. When I looked up the Latina girl had a gun of her own leveled at me. I raised one hand and feigned raising the other when I slammed the automatic gear shift on the floor into reverse. I was now gunning it toward the front doors with no real plan.

The gunman raised his revolver toward my back window but was forced to hesitate. I'd just nailed both garbage cans and sent them his way. He jumped over one and half stumbled over the second. As he was gaining his balance, the clerk cleared the counter and tackled the gunman. I was forced to lock my brakes up so as not to run both men over. The store linoleum was slick under my '65's shoes. I was hardly in control. One or both bodies stopped my tires' momentum. I was half in, half out of the store.

As I got out, the Kia came to life and accelerated backward. She screeched to a halt perpendicular to me. She screamed in Spanish to whom I guessed was her boyfriend or husband. Bonnie and Clyde, they were not. She waved the gun but wasn't really pointing it at anyone or anything in particular. I ducked down to see the gunman pinned beneath my back tires. I couldn't have planned a better outcome. He called me what I believe in Spanish translates to 'homosexual' in English. Who I didn't see was the cashier dude from the store. The woman's screaming became louder and then stopped abruptly. I popped my head up to see the counterman walking around the Kia toward me. He carried two guns in his hands. Those would be the gunman's and his gal's. It was safe to get up. He helped me to my feet.

"The name's Jake. Thanks for the help. Are you hurt?"

"No, not at all. My heart's beating two hundred miles an hour but that's about it. My name's Lou. Lou Crasher." He gave my hand a shake that made me wonder if I'd ever play drums again. Jake only had ten or twelve pounds on me, but he looked far more dangerous than even Hollywood could make a guy look.

"What did you do to my Marianna, you pigs? Marianna! Answer me! Get me the fuck out of here."

"Better pull forward slowly, Lou."

When I sat back in my car the gunman screamed in pain. I pulled off him slowly as directed, then shut the old gal down. Jake hauled the man to his feet, and then came through his jaw with a right. It was effortless, but the man's head flew back and forth as if it were held to his shoulders by a rubber band.

"Jesus, that's one hell of a hook, Jake. Ouch!"

"Hmm," was all he said as he let the man slump to the pavement.

My plan was to play an out-of-work musician fishing for information. I had that same sideman adrenalin-rush feeling in my bones when Dave Abbott knocked over my workplace. This drummer was going to burn him down.

Guys and dolls like me are the guns for hire. Line up the show and we'll knock 'em down. When I get hired for a new show I like to get my hands on the songs as soon as possible and get to work. I'll fly through the tunes quickly and start with the hardest piece. It's often the one they'll ask for in an audition situation. The most exciting part for me is when the most difficult piece is committed to memory. No chart necessary.

In addition to all the types of music one can choose to play, there are also different types of musicians one can choose to be. For example, one might be a studio musician and just cut CD's, jingles and soundtracks. Or one might decide they only play live, or play four-string ukuleles at house parties. One might be a songwriter (where the real money is) and never perform. For the most part, I myself am a sideman. Somebody has some material and they have shows coming up, or a recording date, and they need a drummer, they call someone like me—or me, if I'm lucky.

Candy Striper's place had plenty of parking out front. I eased my ride in and threw the club on the wheel. I checked up and down the block two times before I made my way to the house. Set two thirds of the way back on the small lot was a tiny bungalow. Neighbors on both sides owned identical homes. The only difference was that Abbott's gal owned three large hanging baskets over her front porch. I avoided the third step in my climb as I noticed a full-length split down the center of the board. The song "Poker Face" by Lady Gaga could be heard faintly through the door. I knocked and waited—nothing. I tried again, putting more knuckle into it. The door opened a few inches, the way it does in bad horror movies.

"Candy?" I called. Still, the only sign of life was Lady Gaga.

"Candy?" Louder this time. I felt a little foolish shouting this into a stranger's home, but that was her name. Candy Striper was her full stage name. Some four years before my arrival from Vancouver, Candy was one of L.A.'s hottest exotic dancers. She often made headlines in those days as her show often flirted with the obscene. Various arrests added to her fame. She rarely danced today as Jack Daniels and Father Time teamed up on her and softened her marketability. Nobody's heyday lasts forever, which is why they call them 'heydays.'

"Candy, the name's Lou. I'm looking for Dave Abbott." The door opened all the way. With one hand on top of the door, Candy stood falling out of a black and red kimono. A mini Cuban cigar of the Cohiba brand jutted out of the side of her mouth. She spoke out of the other side.

"What do you want with him?"

"I'm a drummer and I'm looking for a gig, actually."

"Who told you to come here?"

"A bass player."

"Cute story. This bass player have a name?"

"A dude named Colby Stakes."

"What kinda name is that? Sounds like a stage name or something," she said, taking a pull on the cigar.

"I think it's the name his mommy gave him, Candy Striper." I smiled like I was playful. She smiled back. I could see how this woman once caused scores of men to take long business lunches and rush the stages she danced on. Sadly, I could also see the wear and tear the life had taken on her. She invited me in. Her place was bright and cozy.

"You sit in the love seat and I'll sit here." I got the better end of the deal as she walked over to a lime green beanbag chair. I've never looked cool sitting in those things. Before descending onto it she opened the kimono and let it fall to the floor.

"Well?" she asked.

"Ah, Miss Striper, you've dropped your robe."

"Oops," she said with a giggle and molded herself into the waiting beans. "Do you like the view or not, handsome? I'm on the edge of these beans here."

"Candy, I don't care if you were born with it, worked out for it, or paid for it. That body makes me glad to be a man." *Flattery gets one somewhere,* was my plan.

"Ooh baby, don't stop there. Go on."

"But juut just one more, Dollface. I haven't seen a body like that since Pam Grier starred in *Coffy* back in the day!"

"Oh my gawd, can I just tell you how huge a Pam Grier fan I am? I so love her, my gawd." She stared at her ceiling fan, no doubt watching a movie memory.

"What are you doing here again, ah—"

"Lou. I was actually looking for Dave. I was a big fan of Fallopian, as well as Sons O' Bitches' Sons." The S.O.B.S. was another one of Abbott's early bands, which miraculously leapt into my head. "Is he here or is there a number I can reach him at?"

"Yeah, I preferred the S.O.B.S. to Fallopian myself." Her gaze returned to the ceiling fan. Just then a Jack Russell terrier burst through a cat door in the kitchen and headed straight for me at Mach-1 speed. Five feet away from the love seat, the dog took flight and landed in my lap. Candy told me the dog's name was Josey. Josey ran up my arm and began gently nipping at my small hoop earrings.

"Ever since he was a pup, he's been in love with earrings."

"He totally drives Dave crazy. It serves him right for wearing such big ass silver hoops. See, I like your earrings—not too big. Just say 'no' if he bites too hard, Lou."

"How'd you come up with the name Josey?" I asked.

"I named him after Clint Eastwood in the—"

"Outlaw Josey Wales, my favorite Western," I blurted.

"Ooh, first Pam Grier, now Josey Wales! I could just kiss you." She struggled to get out of the bean bag chair, then skipped across the floor to me.

"No, that's okay," I pleaded, but it was too late. She leapt Josey style and landed in my lap. She kissed me all over my neck and cheek. The more I tried to explain that this wasn't a good idea, the harder Josey worked at tearing the earrings out of my head. I've lived in L.A. awhile now, but I still wasn't ready for the dog and stripper act.

Just then, Murphy of Murphy's Law kicked in. "Candy, what the fuck is this?" bellowed a baritone voice from the threshold. Sometime during the excitement, Candy's cigar had fallen on the couch and was still burning. She put her hand on it.

"Holy shit, that hurt, Dave," she said climbing off me. "See what you made me do?"

"Why are you naked with a man in the house?" the voice bellowed.

"Lighten up, Dave. He's just a Pam Grier fan. You could take a page or two out of his book of taste." She marched past him to the kitchen to get ice. Her head barely came up to his sloped shoulders. I took that this was Dave Abbott. I was trying mind-meld with the couch.

"Who the fuck is he?" he asked again, from an inflated chest.

I got up and stretched out a hand. "Name's Lou. I'm a drummer looking—"

I was cut short by a short little punch that sat me back in the love seat. Candy screamed an obscenity from the kitchen. Josey had now completely destroyed the cigar butt and was barking at all three of us. Candy came back to the living room and stared up at Dave. Without looking at me she tossed over a pack of frozen peas. It felt good against my jaw.

"Damn it, Candy, I ain't going for this crap no more, I told you."

"Look, he's just some dumb drummer looking for a gig. And he's a Pam fan, too. Hello, you know about me and Pam."

He scratched his chin and appeared to be looking at his pigeon toes for answers. He looked like Frankenstein's scolded monster, the way he towered over his beloved.

"So, so you're like a Pam fan, man?"

"Pam all the way."

"Sorry, dude, it just looked like you and my gal and the dog were getting it on." I couldn't believe my hearing. Candy slid a little closer to Dave.

"Were you jealous, babe?"

His breathing got heavy. Hers did the same. They grabbed each other and began kissing each other madly. The dog kept barking. Dave's hands explored her body like he'd been at sea for eighteen months. On the one hand I was glad Dave wasn't trying to take my head off. On the other hand, this alternative was sure to make me vomit. With the grace of a pair of camels they hit the floor. I knew where this going, and it wasn't my way. Asking for a job wasn't in the cards. I handed the bag of peas to Josey, who tore it apart instantly.

"Don't make a mess," Candy shouted at the dog. As I crept past, one of Candy's hands, which was running through Dave's hair, shot up with a business card for me to grab. I took it reflexively. It had her name and number on it.

As I was pulling the front door closed behind me, I heard

Abbott's Harley Davidson belt buckle hit the floor. I cringed at the thought. I took the steps two at a time, forgetting about the third step with the crack in it. My leg disappeared to the thigh. Somewhere behind me on a higher step was my other leg. This was clearly a position for a yoga instructor, not me. After prying my leg loose and massaging some life back into it, I noticed that Dave and Candy had come outside on the porch to stare down at me. Candy was once again sporting the kimono and was sucking on a fresh cigar. Her expression read boredom.

Dave said, "I been meaning to fix that step." Candy just "hmphed." Josey came out and licked my face.

"You almost got caught in the middle of that one, huh?" Dave added.

"Yeah, but the stair caught me instead." That got me a laugh. I saw my opening. "So, Dave, any of your projects need a drummer?"

CHAPTER 12

I limped back to my ride. A sore leg and a bizarre L.A. encounter were all I'd gained from the Dave and Candy show. At least I now had a face to go with Abbott's name. I'd need to figure another way at the guy.

A late-model Jeep Cherokee cut me off on Juniper Street. This is not a rare occurrence, and not just because this is Los Angeles. It's also due to my car. People see an older car and they assume it's going to be slow. Who wants to be stuck behind that heap? So, they dart around and in front, leaving inches between bumpers, again assuming that we're moving more slowly than we actually are.

My phone buzzed, causing my face to light up as much as my phone screen when I saw Angela's number. I set it to speaker and tucked it between the sun visor and ceiling—a classic car driver's version of hands-free driving.

"Hey, you, I was just thinking about you."

"Oh really? What part of me Lou?"

"The kissing part. Okay, wait, that was corny; can I try again?"

"Might be a good idea," she laughed.

"I was thinking about all of your parts."

"Ah, lay it back a bit Crasher, you're rushing the song."

"Oh yeah? You lookin' for a slow jam, baby?"

"Now you're gettin' me where we need to go."

"That's what I'm talkin' about."

"But we really need to keep this professional," she said. "At least for now."

"So long as 'for now' is like five seconds. Anyway, this handsome drummer who many say resembles a black James Garner with green eyes—"

"Yeah, I'm not really getting that."

"Liar! Anyway, I have a bona fide lead, a suspect if you will."

"Ooh, that's great, who's—"

Naturally my phone beeped. It showed as an unknown number. Still, private eyes must answer phones. I'm sure that's in the handbook.

"Sorry doll, can you hold a minute? It might be case-related."

"Sure."

"This is Lou."

"It's Dave. You were just here."

"Hey, what's up?"

"Are you free for a gig Saturday? My drummer just flaked."

"Sure, what do ya got?"

"I'm guessing you can handle straight-ahead rock?"

"I was raised on it."

"Cool. It's an easy gig. Single shot, forty-five. No check. Eight tunes, seventy-five meal tickets a dude. No back line. Pack light, the stage is a closet. Downbeat eight."

One forty-five-minute set; no sound check. Seventy-five dollars a man; no drums provided. Bring small drum set; stage is tiny. Eight o'clock show time.

"Covers or originals?" I asked.

"Orig' all the way so we gotta rehearse, twice." He paused. "Maybe once if she pops.

Only one rehearsal if the new guy (me) nails it.

"Ever heard of Sheet Music in Westwood?"

"Yeah, I've rehearsed there before."

"Good, I'll text details."

"And the gig is at?"

"Oh yeah, shit, The Dragon's Lair on Melrose."

"Huh, played there too, no problem."

"All right, swing back by Candy's. I'll leave a CD here for ya…and no dickin' around."

"Got it, and thanks. What's the band's name?" I asked mid-way through my U-turn.

"Boning Joanie."

Dumbass name.

When I clicked back to Angela she was in the wind. I didn't fault her for it. The last time anybody stayed on hold in L.A. was 2001.

CHAPTER 13

Michael and Big Eddie Carruthers hadn't gotten in touch, but it was time to head back to the shop and check on things. When I entered the office a pair of shiny red cowboy boots were kicked up on top of the clutter. The boots belonged to Gladys, Eddie Carruthers' seventy-two-year-old sister. Two things I learned early on about Gladys: one was that to judge her book by the cover was a mistake. This woman had more spunk then I did at eighteen when I thought I had the world by the tail. Two, was that she had a mouth on her that would put some of my old football buddies to shame.

"What the hell happened to you, ya little bastard?" Her voice always sounded full of cigarettes mixed with vintage pennies.

"You're going to have to be specific, a lot has gone down."

"I'm talking about some scrape you claim to have gotten yourself into. My brother told me bits and pieces of it."

"Well, a couple of punks stole the business phone from me. We tussled, and I stole it back. I won, and they lost but I'm not squawking about it either way. How are you doing?"

She gave me her sandpaper on sandpaper laugh before taking her boots off the desk to lean forward. "That's a load of crap, Louis, and you know it. Do you want to know what I think?"

"If I say no do you promise not to tell me?"

"Show some respect, you son of a bitch. I still pack a pretty good left, you know, and from the look of it you're not too good at getting out of the way." She paused and lit a cigarette. "Now here's what I think went down. You probably made a play for one of those two-bit skirts you're always drooling after and she said 'no.' But you persisted like the horny little bastard you are until she finally kicked your little ass silly." Her deep laughter turned into a cough, which seemed to make her laugh harder. I tried to look pissed off but couldn't help joining in as I sat down opposite her.

"I'm bloody choking over here, Louis, get me a drink, for Christ's sake. I'm an old broad!"

It was harder to get out of the chair than I expected but I managed and handed her a Diet Coke. "You're welcome," I nagged. She waved me off.

"Seriously though, did she hurt ya?"

Even though Gladys kept up the "she" angle I knew she was concerned. "I'm fine. She doesn't kick very hard." We smiled at each other as she butted out her smoke. "What brings you by the shop, Granny?"

"Oh yeah," she said, riffling through the file cabinet drawers. "I'm looking for some goddamn Tylenol. I've got a hangover big enough to raise the Titanic."

It was my turn to bust her chops. "Is it really a hangover or did one of your sick little boy toys hit you over the head with a sex toy while trying to escape or something?"

She picked up the Louisville slugger we keep under the desk and came at me like a tornado. "Listen to me you little shit. My men beg for it. They can't get enough of me. Comprende, you little prick. Go ahead. Say something else. Go ahead."

"Okay, okay! Calm down. It was a joke. You're so sensitive."

"Well shit, I told you I was hung over, you little..." She sat down heavily in the chair. "If I didn't feel like crap you'd be begging me to pull this thing out of your ass."

"Hey Gladys, I've got some Tylenol, but you have to say

please."

"Screw it. Gimme."

"Nope."

"Please then, you little prick," she asked, pinching the bridge of her nose.

"Just the please, lady." I loved this. Gladys and I were close, but she was always abusive and I was beginning to worry that I liked the abuse. She picked up the bat again slowly.

"Okay, you big baby, here." I tossed the little pack to her. She knocked a handful back and chased them down with the Diet Coke.

"Hey, go easy on those things. I'm going to need a few myself."

She closed her eyes, put her boots back up on the desk, and with a sigh she spoke in a low tone. "All right, handsome, tell me about this donnybrook of yours, with the details this time. Because I'll be honest with you, you don't seem too bad off. But I just don't see you as the brawling type."

"Fine, but here's the deal. I'll give you the whole story, but I don't want any interruptions. No bull. And for the record I am as tough as I need to be, got it? Good."

And so I laid it out for her like a picnic blanket, omitting nothing. She interrupted me about twenty times, which was half her usual number. In the middle of my reconstruction she opened her blue eyes and put them intently on me. Her look was graver than a no-nonsense Supreme Court judge. When I was done she glanced up at the faded ceiling tiles—the ones that remained, anyway. Half a minute crept by before she lit another cigarette and took a long drag. She mumbled something I didn't catch before pulling the filter off the cigarette. Her tanned face worked into a smile as she took another deep drag.

"Son, what you did was just plain dumb. But don't feel too badly. Your whole generation behaves asininely all the time. You risked your life for a damned piece of technology. A piece of ass I would have understood, kid, but hell, a cell phone?"

"It wasn't the phone so much as they pissed me off. I forgot to mention that one of them spat in my face."

"Butt in like that again and this bat goes you know where. Those punks could have been packin' heat, you moron. I'd be sitting here without any Tylenol, listening to the story from some low-rent, flat-footed cop—and then what? I'd have to notify your kin? And brother if you put that on me I'd resuscitate your butt and choke your lights out. Caesar's ghost, my head hurts! Now get out of here, take some time off. Who knows when these workers will be done."

"I've got something I gotta do."

"Whatever, handsome. I'm going up the road and see if I can't take this edge off."

"You want a drink now? Give it a rest, Glads."

"Stow it, you little pissant. These Tylenol ain't doing Bo Diddley. Whoever heard of buying regular strength Tylenol anyway? Not to mention Diet Coke?" She threw the pack of Tylenol at me, sneered at the drink and headed for the door. At the threshold she stopped and turned back to me.

"Hey kid, I hope you did what you said you did with that steering wheel club. If society is a giant body, then those guys must be from the asshole."

"Thanks, Glads."

"So what are you?"

"Excuse me?"

"You know, what part of society's body are you? Are you the arm? Or the leg maybe?" She had a kid-in-a-candy-store grin on her spa-tanned face.

"Why the heart, of course."

"Hmm. Old Gladys here is the pu-"

"Okay, okay, I get it, I get it. Go get your drink, girlie, and leave the little boys alone." She cackled all the way down the hall.

With Gladys gone I checked in on the workers. In Studio E, the Latino with leather knee pads was laying new carpet.

"Looks good man, *muy bien.*"

"Ah, gracias amigo," he said.

I headed over to D and peeked in on two guys hanging a four-by-eight sheet of drywall.

"Dang, you guys work fast," I said.

"Si, a little tape, a little mud and we're done."

"Cool," I said, and left them to it.

I joined Michael and the two guys installing a brand-new security door. I remember Michael welling up at the destruction of the previous door. He stared, fixated, at the installation, like a father who's been handed his newborn son. An employee from the security alarm company stood with Michael and spoke as they looked on.

"You see there's your problem. The phone box is too exposed. The burglars had easy access. It seems clear they breached the door then cut the line seventeen seconds later."

"Is this common?" I asked.

"Sure is," he said, facing me.

"So it's an easy deduction that the alarm was tripped then the line was cut?"

"Yes, that's what I said."

"So why charge a fee to have a car cruise by if this is a common occurrence?"

Irritation spread to his brow, "Excuse me, who are you?"

Michael began a weak-voiced introduction, but I stopped him.

"You're paid a monthly fee but if you have to leap into action you charge another fee. And if you decide to keep the cruiser at the shop, well, we get robbed. Is that about right, champ?"

"Sir, I don't believe you are the client, so if you don't mind—"

He turned his back to me and faced Michael. I made an exaggerated walk around him until we were face to face.

"Listen, champ, I'm thinking of calling the big boss and suggesting that he dump you guys. I hear the Protek company has a sweet deal going right now."

Concern registered on his face. Michael maintained a per-petual nervous, wide-eyed look. I hauled out my phone and mock-dialed Eddie.

"Have a nice day, champ," I said heading back inside.

"Wait a minute. I think I can, I mean, I can waive the drive-by fee in the future."

I put my phone away and walked up to the adjuster and got into his uncomfortable zone.

"If we decide to stay, and that's a big if, the drive-by fee is gone. We get a two-hundred-and-fifty-dollar Visa gift card—"

"What?"

"Hang on, champ, I haven't completed the trifecta. Big Eddie's rate drops by twenty-five percent for an entire year."

"Anything else?" he asked stepping back.

I stepped closer, "Yes, you've got until the end of the day."

His face took on a rouge tint. His breathing got heavy. He had a decision to make. Does he sucker-punch the uppity brother in the face or make the deal. I was prepared for either action.

"You're an asshole," he said, jerking out his phone and marching to his vehicle.

Michael regarded me as if I were part of Navy Seal Team Six.

"I think he's calling headquarters, Michael," I said.

"That was awesome."

The adjuster walked back to us. "My boss wants to talk to you," he said, extending the phone. I took it and handed it to Michael.

"You good from here, boss?"

He nodded his head up and down and took the phone the way a nine-year-old would take candy.

The adjuster glared at me.

"You know, champ, you should reconsider the 'drive-by' handle," I told him. "It's too gangster. Try mobile surveillance or something neat-o like that."

"Jerk," he mumbled, with a face that said he was sure to call his boss and use my suggestion...and claim it as his own.

I headed into Studio B, which has our crappiest drum set, and dug into the eight Boning Joanie songs. If I could get the songs rocking on a crap drum set, then they'd sound like butter when I laid them down on my precious kit, Sweet Louise, and step one to the Abbott takedown would be in motion. I needed the music to be tight. If the tunes were rough, the mission would be rougher. Then it would be time for phase two of the Dave Abbott takedown.

CHAPTER 14

The songs were locked. I could play them forward and backward. Although, not literally backward, it just sounds cool to say so.

The studio door was thick with insulation. I shoved it open and stepped inside.

"Alex? Keyboard player, right?"

"Yeah, what's up?"

"Nice to meet you, I'm Lou." We shook hands.

We were the first ones to arrive at the Sheet Music rehearsal space. We engaged in the usual musicians' small talk, which is basically an exchange of each other's resume. The key to this game is to bring an attitude of total nonchalance, while making sure the key points of your musical past are heard by the other party. If it is done correctly, it comes off as a casual job interview. You just want the other guy to have confidence in you. If this ritual is done with too much attitude, then you come off as a desperate guy who probably hasn't done half of what he says he's done. If both parties bring too much 'tude, then the pleasant interview becomes a dog-pissing contest, or a "my-drums-are-bigger-than-your-keyboard" situation.

The rest of the guys dragged in as coolly as they knew how. When I asked about the trudging, although not in those words, they explained that they'd been out drinking the night before.

We slammed through the tunes for seventy-five minutes straight before some of the boys demanded a smoke break. We were all happy with the break, for it wasn't the length of time that was getting to us; it was the non-working air conditioner in a tight room that was doing it. Fresh air was a nice slap in the face. I couldn't imagine throwing cigarette smoke into my lungs at this point...or any point, but to each his own. The general consensus was that I was doing a bang-up job on the tunes.

A couple of my tempos were a tad fast, but I assured them I would reel it in come show time. They hardly seemed convinced because, as rockers, we all knew that if anything, songs tend to move on the fast side, once adrenaline is tossed into the mix.

I took the spotlight off myself by paying some of the guys compliments. It worked like a charm. Always does with the fragile artistic mind. I told them I wanted to check out one of my charts before we got back to the rehearsal. Alex was the lead smoker as far as having half a cigarette butt left to smoke, while the others were at two-thirds. This gave me more than enough time for what I really had in mind. Sonny, the guitar player, had a dark red guitar unit made by the Line Six Company. It looked exactly like the one Angela's guitar player used at my studio. The truth is they all look the same, but I had my serial number page with me. As I saw it, Alex's remaining half cancer stick gave me plenty of time. I banked on none of the other guys coming back into the furnace any sooner than they had to.

Bull's eye! The numbers matched. I was looking at the unit that belonged to Angela's guitar player. What was his name again? It didn't matter, because my name would be Hero.

"What the fuck are ya doin' man?" Sonny must have butted out his cigarette early. I hadn't considered that possibility. It would have been too obvious to hide my serial number paper, so I acted as though it was a music chart. If he caught sight of it, I was done.

"Huh? Shit, you scared me man. Hey, is this one of those

processors that makes your amp sound like the actual Line amplifier?"

"Yeah, it is. What the hell are you doing with it?"

"Ah, my brother's always talking trash about these things, but damn, man, your amp is straight up killing, man! I can't wait to tell Grady." *Grady being my imaginary brother.*

"Yeah, it's sweet all right, but you don't want to be touching other people's shit, man, seriously."

"You're right, dude, sorry." I moped over to the drum set and added the serial number page to my charts.

When Sonny's back was to me I casually took the page off the music stand and shoved it into the bottom of my backpack. When he turned to look at me, my hand came out with my Gatorade bottle. His suspicion seemed to be subsiding.

If he didn't buy my cover, he didn't let on. The rest of the guys sauntered back in, refreshed by air both of the fresh and the nicotine variety. We launched back into the heavy rock-and-roll tunes for another thirty minutes.

"Will we be squeezing in another rehearsal before the show?"

"Naw, Lou, I'm satisfied. Just listen to the CD I gave you a few more times. It'll be cool."

"Cool."

Smokes took flame once again as we stood in the studio parking lot.

"Is this your Mustang, Lou?"

"Yeah, Chaney, that's my ol' gal."

"Sixty-six?"

"Sixty-five, actually."

"Right on. You should pound out those few dents and slap some paint on her."

"Yup." I promised. "When I get around to it."

"Which in musician speak, translates to, 'I'm broke and it is never going to happen.'" Abbott laughed. The boys dutifully followed suit.

"Exactly, you know the deal."

Cigarettes were butted out and replaced by a bowl. The bowl was in fact a glass pipe shaped like Star Trek's Enterprise and packed full of marijuana. I declined, they puffed. Once satisfied they piled into the bass player's cargo van. It roared to life, but the music of Black Sabbath roared louder from its speakers. Over the heavy metal anthem, "Ferries Wear Boots," Abbott shouted, "Chaney, drop me off at home first, you pissant."

"Yeah sure thing fuck-o," Chaney replied. This is what is called male bonding.

His screeching tires were a call to action for yours truly. I hopped into the old gal and turned her over. I was about to embark on my first real-life tail.

I heard countless voices from countless classic films call out, *Follow that car!*

Chaney's tire-squealing was the only speed to the pursuit. The pursuit wasn't quite as slow as O.J. Simpson's white Bronco police chase, but it was in the snail's pace category of chases. What should have been a ten-minute drive from Riley's to Abbott's took almost twenty-five. They did, however, stop at a 7-Eleven to buy beer.

I followed the van down Abbott's street. They stopped in the middle of the block at a quaint little white house with red trim. As luck would have it, a tiny alley on the left jumped out of my peripheral. I couldn't risk driving by, as not thirty minutes earlier my car was a brief topic of discussion. I ducked in and waited anxiously, eyes glued to my rearview mirror. If this turned out to be some sort of shortcut out of Abbott's I was screwed. The van drove past. My heart slowed. The guys, without a doubt, were stoned because the same Black Sabbath song was blaring out the van windows.

I backed out, and this time I did chance a drive-by of Dave's house. I pictured millions of dollars' worth of gear stashed inside. I was going to enjoy burning this guy down, as they say in movies. The end of the street was a dead-end. I hadn't noticed the sign that was, no doubt, at the street entrance. Rather than go right to the end, I elected to do the three-point turn in and out of a neighbor's driveway. As I wheeled the ol' gal to the left she stalled. She never stalls. I turn her over. She breathed life briefly then quit again. "What is it, doll?" Before trying a third time I noticed my gas gauge sitting so far below the E sign that the needle would need binoculars to see the E.

I shouted, "Mother of pearl, Lou, you moron, now you choose to run out of gas? Sugar," I shouted once again.

I don't like to cuss in the ol' gal. I was now smack-dab in the middle of the street, blocking traffic that was sure to come according to Murphy and his darned laws. I leaped out and started pushing. Traffic was not my only worry; Dave could easily decide to walk his dog or take out the garbage or come outside to take the training wheels off of his bicycle.

My '65 was heavy, as they don't make 'em like they used to. That and the slight uphill grade had sweat gathering at my temples. A Latino boy of about ten jumped behind the car and helped me with the last few feet to the curb.

"Thanks, little man, I ran out of gas."

"How about a tip, mister?"

"Shouldn't you be in school pal?"

"Shouldn't you have put gas in your car?" he said cheekily.

"All right, here's two dollars, ya little hustler. And make sure nobody messes with it."

"Gracias, homes," he said and ran off laughing.

I dug a gas can out of my trunk and started walking, but stopped after three steps. I was met by the same problem: how to get past Abbott's house without being seen. I shook, rattled and rolled my brain until a plan emerged. I walked a few houses away from Abbott's and knocked on what my sixth sense told me was the friendliest door.

A man with a deep voice and a trace of a Spanish accent called through the black security door. "What do you want?" I knew he could see me, but I couldn't see him.

"How's it going man?"

"I asked you what you want, man? You can't just roll up on me like this. And I sure hope you ain't selling anything, 'cause I ain't buyin' shit."

"No, I need a favor, which I'll pay you for."

His voice was right against the door now. "Sorry, dude, I ain't got any gas, man. But hey, if you need any body work done, shit, I'll hook you up, bro."

"That sounds good. Ah, but today I just need to cut through your yard and I'll pay you ten bucks." I held it up to the screen. The door opened and a stocky Latino with a purple goatee came onto the porch.

"What the fuck did you do, homes, that you gotta bring your shit to my yard?"

"Let me put it to you this way. Somebody on this block has been getting with my girl. Now I don't know the dude but she's with him right now and I don't want her to see me creeping by with this stupid gas can."

"Dude, sorry. Dude, that's rough, man. Sure I'll take your ten and I'll take another ten, too."

"What? Why?"

"Cause your story's bullshit so I need compensation if any shit comes down on me."

"Fair enough, pal." I gave up the twenty before his price went up again.

"Hold on, storyteller. My cousin's in the guest house in the back of the property. I gotta tell him you're coming through. You don't want to get shot, do ya? Ah, come on, I'm just playing, dude. Relax." He grabbed a cell phone out of his pocket and called his cousin.

"Ortiz, wake up, fool. I gotta buddy coming back. Let him through. Huh? Because, I said so. Plus, he's got ten bucks for you." He folded the silver cell closed and smiled at me with a shiny gold tooth in the front of his grille.

"This also covers my return trip man," I say.

"Okay, okay, take it easy. Just give Ortiz the ten-spot. He was sleeping but he'll be up now that there's beer money coming."

"Right. Hey, you got a card or something? I have a '65 Mustang that needs body work."

"Hell, yeah, I do. Here. We'll give you a good price too, bro, no doubt."

"Thanks. Oh, and I hope Ortiz doesn't buy light beer with this scratch. I'd never forgive myself."

"I'll bitch slap him if he does."

Ortiz could have been the twin brother to the guy I'd just done business with. His hand was out long before I got near to his little stoop.

"This is a return fare, Ortiz."

"Cool."

I was now back in the narrow alley I'd pulled into earlier and heading toward Burbank Boulevard. The nearest gas station wasn't far. Not that I had a lot of dough to put in the gas can. Abbott's street, Lilac, cost me thirty-two dollars. If I weren't on Angela's payroll I'd be steamed to say the least.

CHAPTER 15

Someone pounded incessantly on my door. That ruled out the cops, they pound and announce. Travis? That didn't add up either; he was more of a leap-from-the-shadows type. Or maybe Abbott was here to take me out. I ran to my room, and grabbed the Louisville slugger beside my bed and gripped it with both hands.

"Who is it?" I bellowed from a batter's stance through the hollow core door.

"Open up fool, it's me, Bobby."

My shoulders dropped. I opened the door and my buddy Bobby brushed past me.

"Well come on in Bob."

"Lou, I need your help, bruh. For reals."

He stood at my kitchen table and gripped a chair-back hard in both bony hands.

"It's my girl, Julie, bruh. She's cheatin'. The two-timing bi—"

"Whoa, slow your tempo Bob. Weren't you bragging just last month about some honey you met at the Rapid Transit Bar? You said you rocked her world."

"Yo, forget that shit man, that wasn't nothin'—this is serious. You gonna help me or not?"

"Help you do what exactly?"

"We need to roll up on her, dog. I need you in case, you know, she's with some thick-neck, biceps-having mutha—"

"Ooh, aah, I get to play the goon; I can hardly control my excitement. Look Bob, I'm sorry but your timing couldn't be worse. Ya see, I've got this case—"

"Yeah, yeah we've all seen the Cymbal Crasher movie blood. You're giggin' in L.A., driving a sweet classic and now you got a fine-ass honey for after dark."

"What the hell are you talking about, Bob?"

"You've got this perfect life, dog. Weren't you listenin'? Meanwhile, your boy Bobby needs one little favor and the Cymbal Crasher makes it all about him."

He pointed a skeletal finger at me, "You're selfish Lou, believe that."

"Is that right? Was I selfish the last time you took me on one of your 'she's cheatin' roller coasters'?"

"Squash that noise, Crasher."

"Whatever," I paused and walked to him and put a hand on his shoulder, "Stop all this jazz bro, seriously."

"All right, okay," he said, sliding the chair under the table and eventually putting eyes on me.

"Can we take your car? My tank ain't got nothin' in it but a gasoline memory, bruh."

"Shit on a snare drum, let's go."

As we rolled along Moorpark Boulevard I could almost hear my ride laughing at me. Bob had talked me into another ridiculous venture. He kept asking me to step on it but I ignored him. Not a chance was I getting a ticket for the fool.

We decided parking directly out front was no big deal, seeing as Julie didn't know my ride. The second doors closed, Bob sprinted to a side walkway. I sprinted after him and caught him near a small picket-fence gate.

"Do you mind clueing me in on your plans, Bob? Shit."

"Look, we creep down the neighbor's walk and then I'll show you something. Come on."

An old palm tree grew at an angle from the backyard we stood in, snaked over the fence and into Julie's property. We peeked through the fence but saw only thick vegetation. Bob suggested we climb the "leviathan," as he put it. He held an upturned palm for me to lead the charge. I didn't squawk. I wanted this over with. We were able to do a graceless duck walk for the first section. After that it was a hug and shimmy sort of dance. I knew I should have joined the circus when I was a kid. Below me was an oval-shaped pool that hadn't entertained a swimmer since George W. Bush was president.

"I can almost see into a second-floor bedroom."

"Can you see them?"

"I said 'almost,' Bob."

"Lou, a woman ever let you hold her like you're holding this tree?"

"Quit playing the fool."

"Move a little higher, Lou."

"I don't know, Bob, I think we're at the—"

Without as much as a creak, the old palm snapped. A moment like this gives you just enough time to utter a curse word, make a funny face and take a deep breath. We were heading for the murky waters below. It was only natural to try to distance ourselves from the tree in the interest of future family planning. The noise must have been heard down the block. Palm leaves everywhere. The water reeked. I wondered if this was where the phrase "dirty pool" came from. The pool lights came on. Julie obviously heard the rumpus.

Bob grabbed my arm. I could barely make out his bulging eyes. Bubbles escaped his mouth—panic. Looking up, I noticed an area thick with huge palm leaves. We swam to them. I was now close enough to see that they formed a sort of makeshift tent over the top of the water. I poked my head up and sucked air in quietly. I pulled Bobby into the tent by his shoulder and immediately slapped a hand over his mouth and shushed him.

"Bobby? Bob honey, is that you?"

"Yeah babe," he said, struggling away from me then immediately flailing. I caught up to him and drag-swam him to the shallow end and up the three steps and laid him down. Julie and I stood over his panting body.

"Bobby what the hell!" she said, shoving me aside and kneeling down beside him.

"Are you hurt, Sweetie?"

Bobby gave an academy award performance of squinting the eyes, coughing and rolling in agony. He did everything he could to avoid his woman's wrath—can't say I blamed him.

"What did you two think you were doing? Did you put him up to this?" she asked, looking at me.

"Me? Hell no. Bob, you better start talking."

"Lou said the tree was solid," Bob croaked like an anemic frog.

"You little shit, I'm about to drag you back to the deep end."

"Stop it, Lou, you're scaring him."

"You two are scaring me," I said, taking my shirt off to wring it out. "Tell her why we're here, Bob, so we can get moving."

"Bob, honey," she said, cradling his head in her lap and kissing his forehead, "what's going on?"

Julie was a light-skinned sister with faint little freckles so cute you wanted to put them in a jewelry box and slip it in your pocket. Bob sat up and dropped his victim status.

"Girl, straight up, I know you been cheatin' on me. Don't deny it. I been calling and texting—shit, I almost emailed you."

Julie slapped him on the shoulder. Bob flinched.

"You dummy, I told you about answering your phone."

"Huh?"

I wrung my shirt out a final time, the water dropping around my soaked running shoes.

"My phone died, Bobby. I've been at the Apple store half the day."

"Prove it," Bob said doing his best to inflate his scrawny chest.

Julie slapped him on the shoulder, causing Bobby to flinch a second time.

"I borrowed one of the employees' phones and called you and left a message. Go ahead and check, go 'head."

Bob slowly eased his phone from his wet front pocket. Julie and I eye-rolled in unison.

"Give it to me, I'll put it in rice." Bob handed the phone over. Julie folded her arms. "You do believe me, right? That I left that message?"

Bob nodded like a six-year-old that left the gate open, causing the dog, Rex, to escape.

"And you," she said turning her guns on me. "What were you thinking, climbing a rotten tree like that? Look at this mess."

"Julie-baby I'm sorry about your fine landscape and poolside but you have no idea how badly I don't want to be here." I turned to Bob. "And you brutha, better start your apology tour right now."

"Look here, girl, I screwed up okay; I'm sorry. It's just I've never felt like this over no woman," he said inching closer to her. "It's like you drive me crazy or something."

He gently took her hand and put it to his cheek. Her features softened as she slid her body close to his.

"Baby, I never should have let Lou bring me out here like this; I'm sorry."

I pictured nineteen different ways of killing Bob in that moment. They kissed. When they pulled apart they stared, smiling at a two-hundred-and-five-pound shirtless, wannabe P.I. in bog-smelling Levi's.

"You know what's next, right, Lou?" Bob grinned.

"You can leave out the kiss, but I will take your apology," I said.

"Bob's gonna get some so, ah, watch your step on the way out, bruh."

Julie waved bye-bye to me without a word and walked Bobby toward the sliding glass door. Bob looked over his shoulder and shot me a cocky grin. I pointed at him and mimed snapping his scrawny torso over my knee like dried kindling. He laughed as he closed the door behind him.

I swore that would be the last time I'd take part in one of Bob's missions to nowhere. He'd really pulled me off course. Now it was time to get back to Abbott, and this time I needed help.

By the time I got back to my car my phone was buzzing on the driver's seat. The screen told me Kat was calling. I hustled to get my door open and answer before it went to voicemail.

"You're just the gal I was going to call."

"Oh really? I was just checking in for an update, how goes the battle?"

"Straight to the point, I like that."

"You know me."

"Well, it's a five-round fight. It's the middle of the fourth and Crasher's ahead on points."

"I like the sound of that so long as you don't get knocked out in the fifth."

"Funny you mention that. I could avoid that knockout with good corner men—sorry, corner women."

"So that's why you were going to call, you need our help."

"I'd welcome it with open arms and a two-million-dollar smile."

"Hold a sec, Lou."

There was a five-second pause, then I heard the gym's three-minute bell ring in the background. Kat must have been waiting for it to pass before talking to Tami.

"Yo, Tami, Lou needs our help, you in?"

"Natch."

"You hear that, Lou?"

"Sure did. Don't you want to know the gig first?"

"We're fighters and we're in your corner, just give me time and place."

"Actually, the time is fifteen minutes and I'm coming to you if that's cool."

"No time like fifteen minutes from now, Momma always said."

"Thanks doll," I said. "And Kat…"

"Yeah."

"You know I love you ladies, right?" I said, pouring it on thicker than molasses.

"You'd be a fool not to, a serious fool," she said, killing the call.

I fired up my ride and cranked the heater. I spread my T-shirt over the dash vent as best I could and tucked my shoes up close to the floor heater on the passenger side. One thing about the ol' gal is she doesn't have air conditioning but her heater works like an industrial blast furnace.

I barely crawled three blocks before my soaked jeans drove me to the brink of itchy insanity. I pulled over and shimmied out of my pants, which was no easy task within the confines of a '65 Mustang. I slid my shirt to the right and made a home for my jeans. The dank water mixed with blast-furnace heat made for a pungent dead-animal-in-a-marsh aroma. Good times.

I was slightly concerned about being pulled over by a cop and getting popped for indecent exposure but the itchy-chaffing denims removal outweighed the possible moving violation citation. I still kept my damp boxers on as there'd be no way of talking my way out of "rolling around L.A. in a classic while nude" beef. I was slightly less miserable but, hey, nobody said being a P.I. was easy, certainly not Jim Rockford.

As I eased back onto the road my jeans slid across the dash. I moved them back over the vent and drove one hand on the wheel, one on the Levi's. The stench now smelled like dead possum on a charcoal barbecue.

I pulled into the parking lot of Kat and Tami's gym. The new sign; Total Impact Gym had a large black background and bright yellow lettering. The font was bold and forward leaning, like a locomotive. I was impressed. The building continued its black and yellow theme and its blockish shape gave the feeling you were entering a massive bank vault with police-tape yellow trim. To the right of the front door was a sign boasting what the gym offered: Mixed Martial Arts, Kickboxing, Muay Tai, Self-Defense, Police and Military Combat, Jiu Jitsu and Anti-Bullying for Youths. A one-stop shop of bad assery!

My T-shirt, although smelling off, was nearly dry. I got out to put the jeans on. There was no chance I could shimmy back into them while inside my car.

With one leg in and one out, a mother and her pudgy nine-year-old boy exited the gym. Upon seeing me the mother hugged her son close to her body and quickened her pace.

"Here for the anti-bullying class?" I asked.

The mother kept her eyes dead ahead and ignored me. Her son nodded, which nearly caused his glasses to fall from his face.

"Well hang in there, kid, you've come to the best place in Los Angeles."

They reached a two-tone blue, '90s minivan and practically burned rubber out of the parking lot.

I entered the gym and asked the receptionist for Kat and Tami. I was shown a designated area for guests to observe. The gym had two rings, one a standard boxing ring and the other a mixed martial arts octagon cage. Tami and a black woman with dreadlocks pulled back in a ponytail, worked in the MMA cage. Tami held Muay Tai gloves, which allow the partner to punch or kick as opposed to regular boxing focus pads meant solely for punching.

Tami had the fighter work a jab-jab-cross hand combination into three rapid round- house kicks. The kicks rang loud throughout the gym. I wasn't the only one paying attention. Two guys working their heavy bags turned at the sound of the kicks and stopped to watch. A thickly built Latino stepped beside me.

"I'd rather take a baseball bat to the leg than have Keisha lay that roundhouse on me," he whispered to me.

"That makes two of us."

They'd told me about Keisha, the new up-and-coming MMA fighter. She had turned professional less than two months prior and asked Kat and Tami to train her. The Latino suddenly turned to me with a screwed-up look on his face. Then I remembered.

"Sorry cat, I fell in a sewer this morning."

"Dang, dude," he said, and walked away.

I moved to the farthest corner of the observation area I could find and waited for the final bell to sound. When Tami and Keisha were done they bowed to one another, then hugged. Keisha got down on the mat and began doing post-workout stretches. She made the splits look easy. A few kids from the anti-bullying class watched her through the cage with giant smiles on their faces—Keisha's first groupies. She opened the cage door and invited them in to chat. It was obvious she was a good role model.

Kat and Tami came over. I headed them off at the pass.

"No hugs today ladies, I fell in some skunk water."

The women got close and grabbed their noses.

"Oh my god, you are rancid," Tami said.

"Dang," Kat agreed. "Let's take this outside."

It took ten minutes to bring the ladies up to speed and almost another ten begging them to let me into the Chevy Avalanche.

"We're serious, Lou, we want this vehicle detailed after all of this."

"You have my word, let's go."

On the drive to Dave Abbott's we briefly talked strategy. The plan was simple: get to Dave's and do some surveillance.

"There's his place. And that car out front is his. I haven't seen him drive it, but he was bitching about how hard it's been finding parts for his classic Datsun 510."

"Cool."

We sat five minutes before realizing we had no idea how long we'd have to wait or if we'd get any action at all.

"Lou, seeing as we're out of direct sight line to the house, would you mind—"

"I got it," I said getting out to stand beside the truck so the smell would outgas into the night air.

To pass the time, the women told me, in low voices, about Keisha, the hot-shot female fighter they were really jazzed about.

"I'm telling you, Lou, once we get her ground game up all bets are off. She'll hold the belt for a good long while."

"That's awesome," I said, "she's got confidence in you two, number one. But she'll also be good for business, yeah?"

"Oh yeah, sponsors and promoters have been crawling all over our place like roaches," Kat said.

"Now what about you and this Angela chick?" Tami asked.

"What about her? And remember I never kiss and tell."

"Like hell you don't, you're a red-blooded male," Kat laughed. "Is it serious?"

"Not yet, but I wouldn't be opposed to it," I said hoping to change the subject.

"You're sure jumping through enough hoops for her, I'll say that," Tami added.

"Oh shit," Tami said looking at the house. I ducked down knowing Abbott emerged. He hopped into the Datsun. I eased the back door open and slid inside.

"Ladies, follow the leader and not too close," I said.

"You don't want to search the house?"

"Nah. He moves big stuff and that joint is tiny. Besides, I don't think he'd keep the jazz with him. I'm betting on a storage locker somewhere."

"You're the P.I. in all this."

"Cool, don't get too close."

"No duh, Lou," Kat said tailing the rectangular-shaped tail lights.

We stayed three car lengths back in the adjacent lane. After two lefts and a right he tucked into a Shell station. Kat hovered near the air and water area. I crouched down in my seat. Abbott had just flipped the gas lever down as we got comfortable and was done in seconds. He couldn't have tossed more than three bucks into his ride.

"Probably not going far, assuming he was on empty."

"Cool, that'll save you some gas money, Lou."

I took a damp twenty out of my wallet and placed on the seat. Abbott led us on a straight path from Sherman Oaks to a little dead-end street in Panorama City near the Budweiser brewery. If you weren't looking for it, you'd never know it was there.

The air was thick with the smell of hops and barley.

"I'm going to stop here," Kat murmured. "I don't want us to get pinned down. You run down there and see what the bastard is doing."

"Sure enough," I said and climbed out of the truck. On one side of the street birds of paradise grew the length of a wire fence. I hugged the fence as I kept low and sprinted down the block.

The block ended in a half-circle with ten yards of gravel, which butted up against railroad tracks. Two plain white five-ton cargo trucks were parked one behind the other near the circle's curve. Abbott was parked in front of the first truck. As I closed in on the rear truck, I heard the roll-up door of the first truck fly up.

"Okay, what have we got to fence this fine evening?" Abbott was talking to himself. I could see the back of his left shoulder. He moved a flashlight over the truck's spoils.

"Son of a bitch," I whispered.

There was a rustling sound at the fence behind me. I looked to see a tiny black and white rabbit hop from the birds of paradise.

"Who's there?" Abbott called. His light flew past the truck. He could not see the rabbit from where he was, so naturally he had to investigate. I didn't have time to slither under the truck. Not soundlessly anyway. Up was the only solution. One foot on the tailgate, the next on the side handle and I was on top of the truck lying flatter than a Denny's pancake on my belly. Abbott moved below.

"I said, who's there? Fer chrissake! Aw shit, a fuckin' rabbit. You're fucking lucky I don't have my thirty-thirty with me Bugs-friggin'-Bunny."

He went back to work. I quietly rolled onto my back, took in the stars and drank in the brewery's pleasant odor. Soon after, the door rolled down, Abbott's ride fired up and he was gone. Moments later the Avalanche barreled down the street. Brakes locked up, causing the back end to swing out slightly. I climbed down from the truck roof.

"He passed right by us with a shit eater's grin on his big-headed mug," Tami said.

"Anything happen, Lou?"

"Sure. I don't suppose you have a pair of bolt cutters in that lovely truck of yours?"

"A truck without tools is pretty much just a car, Crasher."

Kat reached behind the truck's seat and pulled orange-handled cutters out. I was duly impressed and said as much. Kat allowed Tami the honors as she said she'd never popped a lock before. She seemed very pleased with the pop sound of the snapped lock.

I rolled the door up.

"Mother fu—" Kat started.

"Yup," I said as we stared at the box—full to the roof with musical equipment.

We lucked out, as most of Angela's gear was at the back of the truck. As we tightly packed Kat's truck, I thought of all the musicians whose gear we were looking at, like the kid who saved his allowance to buy an amplifier. I thought of the street performer who, after collecting a million soda cans, buys an acoustic guitar. My thoughts then moved to the female drummer. She has it bad enough being in this traditionally man's business, and then she has to ask two hundred times a day through a six-inch speaker if she can take our order at the local burger joint. Finally, seven months go by before she buys a priceless vintage snare drum. Stories like these and more could easily be attached to this equipment.

I realized that I wasn't home yet. I would still have to do the gig with Dave just to be sure he didn't put two and two together:

Gear gets stolen, sub drummer doesn't show up for gig. If Dave was just a thief I wouldn't worry, but there were the rumors of his "protection."

I ran it by the women and they agreed with my reasoning. Still, it was not going to be easy to lay down solid grooves with a plastic smile on my face. My only hope was that I didn't hop my kit and drop Abbott like a bad cold.

We popped the lock of the other truck but it was empty. Only Abbott knew when he planned to fill it. We moved down the road like crustaceans attempting to avoid a steaming pot of water until a pay phone came into view. It was a miracle that we found one at all in this day and age, but that's the Valley for you. I jumped out and called the law to report the truck. There was a ton of chaotic background noise. The operator wanted my name and other details, but it was time to fly. We chanced a police cruiser in the area might see us with our truck full of booty but thought it a necessary risk, seeing as the five-ton was now without a lock. No telling what the black and white rabbit might do with all of that gear.

We were quiet as we departed the scene and held the speed limit. No doubt the women felt as I did, that none of us had done something like this before.

"That worked out like a funk-rock track, but we may have a problem," I said.

"What's that?" Kat asked.

"My apartment is too small to store this stuff."

"Looks like it's the ladies to the rescue again, Louis."

"Really? How?"

"The storage shed at the gym is half empty," Tami said. "Just don't plan on keeping it there too long. Cool?"

"The coolest. Cheers."

A little while later we unloaded the gear and locked it up. After touchless hugs and air kisses I climbed into my Mustang, waved goodbye, and called Angela.

CHAPTER 16

Only a fool couldn't read the look on Angela's face when she opened her door for me. She was up for it, and I, not wanting to keep it all for myself, was going to give it to her.

She said nothing, which ironically made her message louder and clearer. It also gave the whole vibe a rock video element to it. I floated across the threshold. One of us closed the door behind me. She grabbed my hand and led me into her apartment. Her toned scapular muscles rippled gently within the camisole-style tank. My eyes moved south, how could they not? Her butt was trim and round and moved as if to an old-school, smooth R&B track. My Levi's began tightening in the party department.

Her kitchen was the same as the last time I visited. But I barely noticed it. I can only guess the furniture hadn't changed much either, as my attention to detail was all Angela, all day long.

We stepped into her bedroom. At the bed she looked back at me over her shoulder with a look I'll never forget. But we continued past the bed. Slightly confused, I followed like a pirate to a siren. Hell, I'd probably have followed her into a wood chipper the way I was feeling.

Once in the bathroom, she pulled off my shirt. I returned the favor with her thin tank then reached behind her and unclipped her bra. She raised an eyebrow, clearly impressed with my dexterity. I gave her a quick, you-ain't-seen-nothin'-yet wink. My slightly unhinged Uncle Curtis, who actually had a mannequin in his basement, taught the bra-removal trick to me.

"Only a sucka lets a bra slow a man from getting' his, Lou, remember that," he said as he counseled me on various bra-brand clasps—unorthodox schooling to say the least.

Angela undid my belt buckle and slid my jeans to the floor, grinning up at me with a look that froze time. She had to do some deft maneuvering to get my boxers over my arousal.

In slick move number two, I got her white lace hip-hugger panties down in a tenth of a second. That got me a second eye-brow-raise. She leaned into the shower and set the temperature just right. With her back to me and her butt winking, I nearly lost...everything but managed to hold in all my lovin'.

We stepped in and took our time lathering each other up. By the time we rinsed, we knew everything about each other. We got out and moved back to the bedroom, kissing and stumbling all the way. Angela lay a big beach towel over her comforter and lay back on it. I climbed on top and eased inside her. She inhaled deeply. Our tongues made their own music as our bodies moved as if to a slow jam until we stepped it up to a mid-tempo rhythm and blues number. I got far into her, her back arching with each deep thrust.

I considered changing our position but didn't want to risk losing what we had. All of her sounds echoed my thoughts. If a guitar solo during a live show sounds dynamite, I'll often signal the guitar player to take it around for another progression. I was planning on taking Angela around for about six progressions, if possible. A lyric from a Jimi Hendrix song popped into my head, "Play on drummer, play on."

And that's exactly what I did. I played as if the Supreme Court were outside her door waiting to send me away for life. I upped the tempo several beats per minute. Angela and I were a kick-ass band, playing my favorite song. I slid my right arm under the back of her left thigh; hiked it up and dug deeper. Her high-pitched moan told me I'd made the right move.

"Oh shit," she said, grabbing the back of my head and pulling my mouth to hers. Her body tensed. She cried out with a shiver right when I blew my stack like a Stax record horn solo.

"Oh shit," I said using her words.

I collapsed panting like a grizzly bear on her tight tiny frame. I moved to get off but she held me close. Who was I to complain?

"That was one hell of a crescendo, Lou Crasher."

"Well, you know what they say."

"Well," she breathed heavily, "what do they say?"

"If you're gonna do it, do it with a drummer!"

When we woke, we both seemed surprised that we'd slept forty-five minutes.

"Dang, Lou, you knocked me out with one shot," she said, sliding over to rest her head on my chest.

"I've got more shots, I promise."

"You're a nut. But seriously, who are you? You're not a real P.I. but you find all my gear and then bang the crap out of me? I feel like we're in a movie."

"Yup," I said, folding my arms behind my head and feeling proud.

She leaned on her side and let her head rest on her hand. She looked happy: sweaty, glistening and happy.

"You really got everything? All of my stuff?"

"All but the guitar processor—your guitar, what's his name—"

"Reggie."

"Yeah, Abbott, that's the guy I've got a gig with, his guitar player has the Line Nine processor so that's that, I suppose."

"Oh no," she said sitting up like a shot, "no, that's almost the most important piece of gear. I told you we're going in the studio soon, right?"

"Uh huh."

"Well that processor has some effects in it that, shit, let's just say that the songs aren't the songs without it. Damn it," she said rolling to her back.

"Really? I was still planning on doing the gig, so I still may have a shot at it."

Shut up, Lou. The sex is making you dumb. No way you can pull it off.

"Really?" She said rolling back over to me. "You can get it back? You'd do that for me?"

"It's what you're paying me for," I said. "And the job's not done yet. Besides, it sounds like your record depends on it."

Didn't I tell you to be quiet?

"Oh my god, you're amazing," she said, climbing on top of me. She leaned down and kissed me slowly.

"So what's the band's name, Abbott something?"

"No, Dave Abbott's the band leader, but the band's obnoxious name is Boning Joanie."

"That is obnoxious." She kissed me again, longer this time.

"Ooh somebody's awake," she said, grinding slowly north and south on me. Once she became satisfied that the time was right, she guided me in.

Dave Abbott woke to his buzzing cell phone. He rolled over, saw the name and hit 'decline.' The phone rang again seconds later. *Fuck!*

"Yeah, what's up?"

"What's up, my ass, Dave," Angela barked. "Why didn't you tell me *you* stole my shit?"

"Calm down, Ang'."

"I won't calm down, why did you take my shit?"

"I didn't, Travis did."

"Well that little shit works for you so why did you let him take—"

"Listen bitch—"

"Excuse me?"

"Listen Ang', Dave sighed. "Travis told me he popped some

dump in Hollywood but he didn't say which dump. If you just sit tight I'm gonna work all of this out. You gotta trust me on this, I've done you damn good up to this point, ain't I?"

Angela fumed. She thought their little arrangement was shaky to begin with—but now this crap.

"I need that guitar processor back."

"Can't do that, Sonny's attached to it, and besides, it sounds bad ass on my tunes."

"Listen to me, you son of a bitch, that effects unit is mine, and I need it back like fucking yesterday. I got a studio date, remember?"

"Not my problem."

Silence.

"Not your problem? Is that how you want to play it?"

"Look, I'll get you another one, or shit; pretty soon you'll have enough scrilla to buy fifty fuckin' processors. And why the fuck are you so obsessed with that piece of gear? Why you ain't asking for the rest of your shit?"

"Because," Angela said through gritted teeth, "I've already got the rest."

"Bullshit, and don't think I won't check my fuckin' trucks, Ang."

"Good. Run and check your trucks. Run sucka, run," Angela said, before the line went dead.

Dave slammed his phone on the bedside table and swung his legs out of bed.

"Fucking bitch," he said, hauling open the top drawer of the side table and pulling out a bag of cocaine.

"Who's a fucking bitch? Better not be me," said Jasmine, an attractive Indian girl.

Jasmine was beautiful and what Dave referred to as his side action. She was way too hot for his league, and he knew she came around for his blow, which was no big deal, because he had her around for the tail. *Everybody wins.*

"Ah, just some dumbass singer bustin' balls."

Dave dipped a spoon into the bag and hit each nostril one time.

"Puff, puff, pass," Jasmine said, using an old pot smoker's phrase.

"This ain't pot, Sugar."

"Then toss that lovely bag and spoon this way before I get pissed."

"Fuck," Dave whispered, handing her the stuff.

Jasmine bumped a little more than Dave.

"Whoa, slow your roll, Hoover vacuum."

"Well you're so stingy I don't know when I'll see it again. And look here, I'm no vacuum. Your girl Candy though, ha, that girl is an industrial shop vacuum."

"Hey," Abbott shouted, grabbing Jasmine hard by the wrist. "You don't talk about her, ya got it? Never!"

"Ouch, fuck, okay."

Dave let go and began coughing, hacked a loogie into the trashcan and got dressed. As he headed for the door, he called, "Don't go running through that coke, Jaz, I know how much is there!"

"Fuck you too, sweetheart."

Dave was pissed. The Angela call, the Crasher angle, something was fucked. Dave didn't like it when things were fucked. He hauled out his phone as he headed to his car.

"What up?"

"Travis, I'm gonna text you an address."

"What address, for what?"

"We need to move my trucks," Abbot said, irritated. Travis was quiet a moment.

"Yeah, I know I never told you where they were; well consider yourself moved up the ladder."

"'Bout fuckin' time."

"Stop at the nearest place and pick up a couple of good padlocks. I expect you there in thirty. Drop hammer. If you get a ticket, I'll cover it."

"Shit, Dave, I never would have known this little hideaway was here," Travis said. "That's the idea, shit-bird," Dave said, approaching the truck and noticing the dangling broken lock. He'd never told Angela where his trucks were—never told anybody.

"Fuck," he said, pulling off the lock and raising the door. He could tell at a glance Angela's gear was gone. Even if she'd followed him out here at one time or another, he couldn't see her climbing around a truck, looking for shit. No, she'd had help. The bitch wasn't bluffing, but she'd definitely pay.

"That's a shit ton of gear, Dave."

"There's a lot more where that came from, Travis."

"So why ya pissed?"

"Cause some of it's missing—enough with the questions. Throw the new locks on and follow me out. I'll drive this one." Abbott gave Travis hard eyes. "You told me you got your air brakes license, is that true or were you bullshitting?"

"My old man was a trucker, what do you think?"

"Good. Take this one," he said, handing Travis the keys. We'll park at a new spot I got picked out and uber back—your app.

The spot was in an industrial area on Valjean Street not far from Sherman Way in Van Nuys. They got the trucks settled and were back out to the little street behind the brewery in under forty minutes.

"Move your ass," Dave growled, noticing Travis casually firing up a smoke before getting into the Caprice.

"What th' eff, Dave?"

"I want us both out of here. You want to move up the ladder or not?" Dave stepped forward, towering over Travis.

Travis hopped into the Caprice with a curse and fired up. Dave did the same and pulled out, leading the way. After the first right, he checked his mirror. Five seconds after Travis made the turn, two cop cars crossed through the light and headed down the street to where the trucks had parked previously. Shit!

Dave hoped Travis hadn't seen the black and whites. Didn't

want the little tough guy getting spooked. He cursed again.

Twenty miles later, Dave signaled Travis to pull over. He stood outside his car with it idling. Travis got out with a freshly lit butt.

"Good work, Trav. Now remember what this means. You and I are now the only guys who know where the trucks are. So if I get hit…" he paused to close the distance, "…guess who I'm coming for?"

To Dave's surprise Travis closed some distance of his own. "You need to fuckin' trust me, Abbott, how many times I gotta fuckin' tell ya?"

Abbott wanted to laugh at the little pissant's toughness. Why were short guys always like that? Without a word he got into his ride and drove off.

That taken care of, Dave hauled out his phone and called Sonny, his lead guitar player.

"Hey, shithead."

"What's up, fool?"

"That Line Nine processor I gave you, you like it, right?"

"Fuckin' love it, why?"

"It's causing me grief so I gotta charge ya three bills if you want to keep it."

"Fuck, seriously?"

"Seriously."

"All right hold back fifty on our next show then I'll put together the rest."

"Fine. It's all good otherwise? Nobody asking about it or eyeballing it?"

"What, the Line Nine? Nah, well, that drummer, the Crasher dude, was checking it out but he was cool—he's got a brother or some shit that plays, so it's kosher."

Dave had been pinching the bridge of his nose with his eyes squeezed shut until he heard Sonny's words. His eyes popped wide.

"What? A brother who plays, you said?"

"Yeah, why?"

Dave didn't like it. He didn't believe in coincidence, and he didn't like dots connecting. Crasher's name was popping up too damn often.

"Nothing. Just keep your shit tight."

"Whatever that means."

"It means keep your shit—look, I'm going to take a hundred off the Boning Joanie show and I'll need the other two by next week."

"Jesus, the gift that keeps on fuckin' giving."

"L.A.'s got a shit ton o' guitar players, Sonny, remember that."

"Whatever, dude."

CHAPTER 17

Next morning, the ol' gal and I rode in silence back from Angela's. I was of two minds. The first mind sat somewhere north of cloud nine. I hadn't expected us to move as quickly as we were. Heck, from the day she walked into my work joint I thought she was out of my league, but now look at us. My second mind was that I'd bitten off more than I could choke down. How in the hell was I going to steal what had already been stolen? Another fine mess, Lou...

I needed to think and needed to do it fast. I generally like working out ideas from behind my drum kit but I wasn't feeling up to driving to Burbank where my studio sits. Instead, when I got home, I changed into my workout gear and jogged to the little park nearby. The park is postage-stamp sized but has a decent workout area with chin-up bars, a balance beam, ropes and so on.

I warmed up with a five-lap jog then switched to short wind sprints. These include sprinting backward, bear crawls, side shuffling and a few other things that make one feel uncomfortable enough to categorize as fitness.

All the while, I brainstormed on a way to relieve Sonny of the guitar unit. I began with the simplest yet worst plan and that was a ski mask, a smack to the noggin and hightailing it to the reliable ol' gal. The plan was direct but risky. Movies made it look easy to knock a fellow out with a lead pipe, but the danger is that a little too much zeal and one could end up with a corpse at his feet.

After my sprints I moved over to the little outdoor gym. I climbed onto the balance beam and did thirty-five squats. Next were a dozen chin-ups and then on to the rubberized ground area for twenty-five pushups. The last item on the Crasher rock-n-roll circuit was back to the four-foot-high balance beam. I hopped over it a dozen times.

During the hops, I abandoned plan number two, which involved me tailing Sonny home after the gig, following him into his house and hitting him with a chloroform rag from behind. I'd be risking the same problem, being that I'm not time-tested in drugging people. How much juice goes into the rag? What if the cat cashes out? Besides, I wouldn't know where to buy that stuff. Although I've no doubt Jake could supply me with it, I know he wouldn't.

My circuit was complete after the hops. I repeated the whole circuit three more times before heading home with a skeleton of a plan that unfortunately involved the help of my friends. I was running up a serious debt with them but hoped I could make good.

My kitchen table was too small for Kat, Tami, Jake and me, so we gathered in my living area. The lot turned me down on sandwiches, which forced Tami to scour my cupboards and come up with a decent platter of cheese, crackers, cold cotto salami, thin-sliced turkey and prosciutto. I masked my inner cringe at the use of my sandwich particulates. The ladies had tea while Jake and I had Korean beers, Kirin.

"Thank you all for coming and helping a brother out."

"Somebody's got to back you at that Dragon's Lair club so you don't hurt yourself."

"I'm rolling in the aisle, Tami. Moving on. As you know, we're after the 2QXJ5 Line Nine guitar processor."

"What do they go for new?" Kat asked.

"About eleven hundred. The version Angela's guy plays is nearly two years old and could garner seven-fifty to eight hundred."

"So the question is how do we separate the electronic toy from the guitar player?" Kat asked.

"Choke him out," Tami said.

"Too many witnesses," Jake said.

"Do it in the men's room. Can you handle that, Lou?"

"Yes, but you're supposing the cat needs to go. If not, I'd have to drag him in there."

"We could roofie the guy," Kat said. She got our attention. "Not that I know where to get that sort of thing," she blushed.

"Lou's a musician, he's probably got some here," Tami smiled.

"I resent that."

"Why don't we get him drunk?" Kat added.

I loaded up a cracker with sharp cheddar and salami, knocked it back, and chased it with a healthy pull of beer.

"We're actually on the same page here now," I said. "The best time to snag the piece is at the end of the show during load out."

"Yes," Kat perked up. "Either Tami or I will make sure he gets buzzed for the show and then we'll really turn him up when you're done because you guys always drink after your shows right? I've seen it."

"Some of us drink before, during and after," I said. Jake scowled at me.

"Smarten up, Lou," Kat said. "He's looped, we invite him down for shots and then we lift the Line Nine processor, is that it?"

"We need a duplicate—shit that's no good," Tami said.

"No, you're onto something. We just need a duplicate hard-shell case that we load up to weigh the same as if the real deal was inside."

"Load it with what, rocks?" Kat asked.

"Phone books, whatever."

Tami asked the name of the unit again, then pulled it up on her phone after I told her.

"Here," she said turning the phone around. Jake took it from her.

"I'll handle the case and contents," he said, handing the phone back.

"Don't you want me to send you the link or something, Jake?"

"Already got it, Tami," he replied.

Tami raised her eyebrows, clearly impressed by Jake's methods. Kat took the tray back to the kitchen and fixed another platter for us. As she sat down, she smiled at her buddy.

"Tami, I think you should be the bait. We'll make sure we get a table close to the stage so you can work your magic on him during the show. When he's done it should be you flirting and drinking with the guy, you're better at this stuff than me," she paused. "And that's a compliment by the way."

Tami struck a sexy pose, fluttered her eye lashes and said, "Who me?"

"So that's settled," Kat went on. "We need a point between the stage and the parking lot. What do ya got, Lou?"

"Long hallway off stage right. Musicians load in and out through it. Maybe we could stash the replica outside the back door by the dumpster or there's also an ice machine. The case would fit under that as well."

"Dang, you got schematics too?"

"Nah, just played there about twenty times. But speaking of schematics," I said, grabbing a pen and paper.

"Who got an A in art class?"

Jake reached over and took the pen and paper without a word. He asked where the stage was, and I told him.

"Dimensions."

"Thirty by ten deep. Two steps from the floor up to the stage, on stage right, which is left if you're looking from the crowd."

"Tell me things I don't know, Louis. The stage is three feet high, say?"

"About right."

"Hallway."

"Off stage right as mentioned, thirty-five, forty feet long and narrow, we're talking bass drum carried sideways is the only way down that puppy."

Jake drew the hallway free hand with perfectly straight lines. At the end he wrote "exit," then he drew a parking lot.

"Put the dumpster there," I said pointing.

"Cool, now come back down the hall and put a small ice machine here. Good."

Jake wanted to sketch the entire club. While I gave him directions, the ladies grabbed more tea. When Jake was done he asked a final question.

"How many bouncers on weekends?"

"Let's see, always two on the front door, one on the back and three or four floaters."

Jake wrote "security: 6,7" and circled it. I turned to Tami.

"Tami baby, what's your approach?"

"Eye contact during the show. I'll dance in front of him, shake my money maker then when he comes down I'll ply him with shots, something clear."

Kat and Tami exchanged a conspiratorial eye.

"What gives, ladies? Spill it."

"I won't be drinking booze. The bartender will pour me water while Sonny downs the sauce."

"How ya gonna swing that?" I ask.

"I'll go in early and set it up with the bartender."

"So you know this bartender?"

The co-conspirators grinned again.

"They've done this before Lou," Jake said impassively.

"Your words, not mine," Tami said, reaching out and giving Kat a high-five.

I was nearly all out of grub for further trays. The crew didn't seem to mind. I had plenty of beer, though, and pushed them to the point that the ladies broke down and had one each. We decided that as Tami kept Sonny busy at the table, I'd grab his case and shove it to the side of the stage—nonchalant, as if it were my own. Kat was to run interference and fend off anyone that needed fending.

I'd bring an extra floor tom case with the replica inside. When the coast was clear I'd put the fake on stage near Sonny's guitar amp. Then I'd drop a packing blanket over the real processor and leave it right at the edge of the stage.

"You sure you can swing that, Lou?"

"Tami, pack-up is total chaos. You've got band members, occasional fans and soundmen running around, all feeling that their job is the most important. They won't see a thing."

"Cool, so I'll grab the blanketed unit and stash it under the ice machine," Kat said. "Then I'll wait a beat and come back to the club. That way it'll look like I took some piece of gear out to your car."

"Exact-a-mundo, and on my way out, I'll slide the genuine article into my tom case and load it into my ride with the rest of my kit."

"Sounds like a winner," Kat said.

"Tami, under no circumstances are you to allow Sonny to open that case. If he does, we'll have to brawl our way outta the joint."

"He won't, I'm that good."

We all seemed pleased with ourselves. The girls were about to allow themselves a second beer. Then we noticed Jake was solid still.

"Another beer Jake?" I asked.

He nodded.

"So what do you think?"

"A plan is hope for a positive outcome. This plan has a lot of moving parts—a lot of time windows."

"But do you think it will work?" I asked.

"As I said, there's always hope."

"Dang Jake, you say little and give up even less."

"I'll be where I need to be, if you need me."

Confused, hell yes, but I was glad Jake was on our team. Kat and Tami's expressions echoed my inner thoughts.

After pulling into the Dragon's Lair parking lot I locked up the ol' gal and headed toward the club's back entrance. Doug the bouncer recognized me and gave me a fist bump before unclasping the ridiculous velvet rope for me to enter. The hallway was exactly as I'd remembered it. A bar-back with a bright green Mohawk loaded ice into a plastic bucket. I gave him a 'what's up?' and squeezed past.

A heavy rock band with Led Zeppelin-style grooves fronted by a six-foot-six female singer was pumping. Screeching lyrics from the stage, she looked as though she engaged in crossfit regularly. She happened to be near my end of the stage when I came in and pointed at me with a smile. I gave the point right back to her. We didn't know each other from two holes in a wall; it was merely musician-speak for "what's happenin' fellow muzo?"

I did a "once around the park" in the club. I always do a lay-of-the-land lap at a gig. If I get a chance, I'll do a quick "sup brother" to the soundman, seeing as he's the cat that can make or break a show.

The soundman was a heavyset middle eastern-looking cat with dyed blond hair and an oversized nose ring in his left nostril. I shouted over the band that I was drumming for Boning Joanie. I got a nod and a fist bump. We were good.

My belly was crowded with butterflies, and not because I had a gig. This was all about the caper we were about to pull.

I gelled with the crowd for most of the opening band's set. I always like to see what is going on with other bands. There was a lot of buzz about Dave's band floating through the throng. The neat thing about being a sub drummer is that nobody knows who you are, and you can hear what cats have to say in a fly-on-the-wall sort of way. Two tall girls in matching three-inch heels and identical fishnet stockings that ran up to similar black miniskirts talked about Abbott.

"Yeah, it kind of sucks though, because I heard the regular drummer Randy or Andy or whatever quit and the new guy sucks."

"Oh my god really? That blows. I loved Andy/Randy what's-his-name. Let's do a shot so we can stomach this."

"Not true, the new guy rocks," I piped in.

"Excuse me?" one of the ladies responded.

"Yeah, his name's Lou and I hear he went to Harvard."

"So what, they don't teach you how to rock and roll at Harvard." They both had screwed up looks on their faces.

"That's just it, ladies, he taught them how to rock at Harvard and now ya can get a master's in rock at Harvard. No lie," I lied.

"No shit. Is he cute?" the girl who had been silent up to this point asked.

"Well, I hear he's a black guy who kinda looks like James Garner."

"Who's that?"

"Picture Johnny Depp, only hotter, and you've got a young James Garner. You dames enjoy the show."

"Wait, come and do a shot with us."

"No can do, fishnets, I've got a show to do." I winked Sinatra-style and oozed into the crowd.

I heard one of them say 'Huh?' to my back as I walked away. I went backstage and started warming up. I have a little practice pad, which has a thick rubber surface and on this I go through some snare-drum rudiments—which are to drummers like scales are to a pianist.

Ten minutes later I was counting in the first song. My adrenaline was way up, which I expected. As soon as I heard the tempo of the first lyrical line, I knew I was moving this train too fast through a narrow pass. To slow down too quickly is amateur because even the most lay of listeners can feel that. So the choices are either carry on at the speed you are moving and apologize to the boys in between songs, or gradually pull the tune back a few notches. I chose the latter and got a nod from Sonny, the guitar player.

They had me go straight into the second song over the applause from the first song. These types of transitions aren't always easy when you're playing new material, but the switch came off hitch-less. If only the same thing happened moving from song two to three. I was to play a huge Phil Collins-style drum fill over the big toms by myself and then boom—the boys come in on beat one. I dropped my stick just before the fill and was forced to do it one-handed. In the blink of an eye, what should have been the thunderous drums of Navarone became more like the sound of a one-legged mouse, tip-toeing across highly tuned tin pots. However, with my free hand I did manage to throw up the rock-and-roll sign.

I recovered fairly quickly and finished out the set. Obviously with more rehearsal time I could have murdered Abbott's tunes, but such is the life of a sub. Bottom line; it was me in the chair on that night, not some other cat. Respect it and move on, I always say. We were the last band and the club still had another hour of booze peddling time left so there was no rush for us to haul our gear off the stage. I walked through the crowd and received slightly fewer sneers and headshakes than I did pats on the back and glass raises. Ah, the life of a sideman. A short person in a loud satin shirt on his way out of the bathroom held the door for me.

"Thanks man," I said.

"Sure. Nice set, brother."

When I was done I moved through the crowd to the table Kat and Tami had up front. Jake didn't sit. He found various walls to lean on and caverns to hide in. The times I caught his movement he reminded me of a lion moving through tall grass on the Serengeti.

"So, are we ready to drop the hammer on Sonny the guitar player?" I asked.

"You pick a hell of time to doubt us, drummer boy."

"Nobody doubts anybody, Tami," Kat said, rushing to my defense. "Lou's just adrenalized."

"It's almost time to rock, so pay attention, Lou. As long as you do what you're supposed to do, when the time comes it'll all be gravy, as you often say. You know the rest."

She rose up from the table. "And now if you're through with your panic attack..." Tami winked and moved with soul music in her hips toward the bar.

Sonny's back was to us, elbows resting on the bar. Tami eased in behind him and gently rubbed his back. He turned. His confused look morphed into a giant smile when he saw Tami. A firm body with curves in the right places, black stilettos, tights to match, a mini skirt just mini enough, a sheer black top with cap sleeves, long flowing hair and a beautiful smile will do that to any man.

The bartender beelined to the two and took their order. He then reached into his well and pulled out a bottle and poured out a shot. He made as though the spout was blocked on shot number two and worked on it briefly. Tami stroked Sonny's cheek with a slender hand. Sonny moved in for a kiss, but Tami gently turned sideways putting a hand on his chest. That was when the bartender came up with a second bottle with the same label as the first and loaded up the second shot. Tami grabbed the shot, downed it, then made a bitter-taste face. Sonny laughed.

"Bartender's slick," I said.

"Yeah, he is."

Tami immediately held up two fingers to the bartender. Back at our table it was as if the waitress in a black bra, black ripped jeans and heavy eyeliner read my thoughts. She put a beer and a shot of tequila down in front of me. On her left breast was a tattoo of a woman who looked a lot like the waitress herself with a dialogue bubble coming from her lips that said, "Take me."

"Well thank you kindly, how much?" I ask.

"No charge," she said. Tami had sent it over. I did what came naturally with the shot and chased it with a healthy portion of beer, then tipped the waitress three singles.

"Kat, I'm heading to the stage to make a mess of tearing down my drums and do what needs doin'. Wish me luck."

"You got it," Kat said.

Dave Abbott wiped the post-show sweat off his brow and surveyed the club. The gig was cool, and Crasher played all right, other than a few hiccups. There was nothing to pin on him, nothing at all, but still, that didn't mean the dude was innocent. Dave had done well up to this point by paying attention to inner radar, and the radar found something screwy about Sonny's new black chick shooter-drinking buddy. A, she was too hot for Sonny and B, she was a friend of Crasher. She was too into Sonny and could hold her liquor way better than he could. Abbott didn't buy her drunk play; she laughed too much. Sonny wasn't that funny.

Maybe she was just trying to get laid, or maybe something else. More than a few times the bartender fucked with the bottle before pouring out the broad's drink. Dave set up shop at the end of the bar and spent his time watching the two of them while occasionally checking out his new drummer.

The hot black chick ordered another round of shots. She was hot but, holy shit, the bartender did something, he was sure of it. After putting the bottle into the well, the man raised his eyes to Dave, then quickly looked away. He seemed nervous. The hot chick put the glasses on a tray and guided Sonny toward her table. Dave fell in behind.

Standing over the table, Sonny reached for a shot but the hot chick moved him toward the other shot. Bingo, this bitch was up to something. Dave got the visual attention of the bouncer named Rudy, good dude. Rudy, like a loyal dog, cut through the crowd and headed for Crasher's table.

My drums and cases were spread all over the floor, which is out of the norm for me. I'm usually way more organized, but sleight of hand called for strewn percussion gear everywhere. I noticed Dave Abbott tailing Tami from the bar. He looked pissed. Jake walked past the stage and headed down the hall without so much as glance in my direction. The bouncer, Rudy, who is the only bouncer I'm not a fan of, carved through the crowd with pace, heading to my table.

"Shit," I mumbled. Something was about to go down. A scene was about to go down.

Kat was making her way back from the bathroom and from her vantage I figured she could see the scene unfold. I was ready to hop off the stage and do my part. Kat quickened her pace. Dave was directly behind Tami. Sonny, now on wobbly legs, reached for a shot when Tami flirtatiously guided him to the other shot glass. A drummer sees all from the stage.

Dave reached around Tami to grab the shot as Kat arrived in time to bump Dave's shoulder hard. The glass dropped and shattered on the dance floor. Both Dave and bouncer looked pissed. That was it, this game was over. I climbed off the stage and strode toward the group.

I felt a slight breeze as Jake blew past me, walked to the bouncer and whispered something in his ear. He quickly cupped a hand over Dave's ear and obviously repeated what Jake told him.

"Fuck," Dave said, moving fast for the exit hall with bouncer in tow.

Sonny was hammered and oblivious. Jake blended back into the crowd like he'd never been there. Kat and Tami gave me a look like the heist was still a go, so I did a one-eighty and hopped back onstage. Sonny had unplugged his processor, put it back into the case, but left it and his guitar and amp onstage, all thanks to Tami. I pulled a blanket from my bass drum—kept there to deaden the high notes—and dropped it over the Line Nine. Keeping an eye on Sonny, I used my heel to slide the processor to the edge of the stage.

With my back to the dance floor I yanked the replica out of my spare tom case and inched it back to where Sonny's stolen unit previously sat. With Tami in his lap, giggling at every word, he didn't see a thing. Kat eased up to the stage, wrapped the blanket tight around the unit, and carried it down the hall. As she came back, I moved to the edge of the stage. There, she kissed me on the cheek as a dutiful drummer's girl would and mentioned that the processor was actually inside the icemaker.

"Really? Why?"

"There's too much crap under the machine, buckets and stuff."

She kissed me again before heading back to the table. I grabbed my empty tom case and a snare drum case and walked into the hall. My heart rate elevated slightly as the barback I'd seen earlier in the night was pulling the guitar unit from the ice maker.

"What the fuck is this?"

"Sorry dude, that's mine, sorry," I said hurrying over.

"What the fuck did you put it in here for? This is totally unsanitary, dude."

"I know, my bad, it was just that it really heated up on stage and—"

"We make drinks with this ice dude, I gotta tell Rudy."

I put my stuff down and opened my wallet. "Here's fifty bucks. Let's leave Rudy out of it, huh, pal?"

The kid looked at the bill and mulled it over briefly. He'd have to go for it. Barbacks are the lowest on the tip-money totem pole. Finally, with a heavy sigh, he put the fifty in his front jeans pocket.

"Thanks champ, it won't happen again."

He walked away shaking his head. I didn't waste any time

shoving the real processor into my tom case and sealing her up. I grabbed my snare and headed outside. As the fresh air hit my face I realized what Jake had done to cause Abbott and the bouncer to bolt outside.

Abbott's car alarm was going off non-stop. Contents from his glove box were strewn all over the pavement. Rudy the bouncer scrambled to pick up the pieces while Dave cursed with all his heart at his broken driver-side window.

I stood beside Doug the bouncer and took it all in.

"Couldn't happen to a nicer guy," Doug said sarcastically.

"I couldn't agree more," I said. "I suppose you didn't see anything."

"Was on my break," he said with a wink. I knew Doug well. He hated Abbott and Rudy, for that matter. Why you playin' with his ass Crasher?"

"Workin' something," I said, and walked to my ride, where I loaded the two items into my trunk. Then I walked over to Dave and put on a show.

"Holy shit what happened, man?" I asked.

"What's it fucking look like Crasher? And now this fucking alarm won't fucking stop, fuck!"

I would have bet a hundred bucks that the battery in his key fob was dead or dying, thus, the alarm was going to party all night long. Those things are no different than a TV remote. But I wasn't going to tell him. I liked watching him lose it. He deserved it.

I went back inside and gave Kat an exaggerated wink, then continued loading up the rest of my drum kit. We were in the home stretch of our plan. I had what they call a six-piece drum set: a snare drum, bass drum, three rack toms and one floor tom.

Your standard drum kit usually consists of five pieces. And back in days of the American jazz cats, one would usually see four drums to a kit. The hard rockers of the late seventies and eighties bumped it up to seven, eight and sometimes nine-piece and more. Keep in mind the drummers of those sets usually had drum techs, roadies, managers and a gal in every port. At my level, with the music I play and the size of my classic ride, a six-piece is just right.

As I tossed each drum into a separate case, I glanced as inconspicuously as possible at Tami and Sonny, who were now onstage with me, helping to pack up gear. Abbott didn't pack his own. Instead, he had some wide-eyed fan that must have had a fake I.D. do his grunt work. The fan seemed happy to be getting a foot into the rock world, or so he thought. He totally ignored us, pausing only to push wire-rimmed spectacles back up onto his nose as they repeatedly headed south. I packed all my stuff and set it by the side of the stage.

Sonny swayed slightly as he asked me to help him lift his amplifier off the three-foot-high stage. He brought his side of the amp down on his toe and cussed. Tami tried to stifle a giggle. Sonny, red-faced, smiled at her, telling her she was cute. I wanted to puke, but this was not the time. As I walked down the narrow hall, Sonny instructed Tami to leave the rest of his stuff where it lay. Musicians are typically protective about their gear, even if recently and illegally acquired. No doubt he envisioned Tami taking a dive with his new toy.

Tami came out the door like a woman attempting to not appear drunk, with Sonny's guitar in tow. Either she had an acting background, or a drinking background, or both, because she was good. Sonny hurried up from behind her with short little steps.

"Baby, watch the axe. You shouldn't have brought the—"

Tami planted a big kiss on his lips to cut him off. He broke free from her when he heard his axe hit the pavement. The guitar was okay, as it was in a hard-shell case. Abbott's alarm was still going off, but it had slowed and sounded like an old vinyl record winding down on an unplugged turntable. Perhaps his car battery was dying. Good. Rudy stood, shifting foot to foot, as if awaiting instructions.

As I came back from my car I stopped at Doug and the velvet

rope. "So does that Rudy fool work for the club or for Abbott?"

"Exactly. We usually stick around for a beer after hours. Tonight, I think I'll skip the beer and just punch Rudy in his liver."

"Cool," I said, unsure what else to say.

Back inside the club I hopped back onstage and did what we players call an "idiot check," where we make sure we haven't left anything behind—like an idiot. Satisfied with the check, I turned to see our table was empty with chairs up. I spotted Kat and Jake at the bar. Jake hugged Kat and he made his exit. Let the record show that I was not hurt that he didn't say goodbye to me. I'd see him soon enough.

"Hey, Kat. The switch came off without a hitch. Now I guarantee Sonny's going to want to keep the party going with our gal, so how do we get her out?"

"We've got that all worked out."

"Oh yeah? I'm listening."

"Well you can listen outside," a bouncer I didn't know interrupted, "'cause we're all closed up. You don't have to go home but you can't stay here."

"Awesome movie wasn't it man? The Blues Brothers movie. That line, I think John Belushi said it," I said.

"Dude," the bouncer said. "I've only seen it like fifty times. It's a classic. Hey, nice playing tonight bro. Try to wrap it up in five."

"Cool."

"Let's move it outside, Louis," Kat said, "and I'll give you the plan."

We moved out back to my car. No sign of Tami or Sonny. A pile of broken glass lay where Abbott's car had been parked. I now had all of the pieces to Angela's inventory. I was feeling good.

"They've split, now what?" I asked.

"She's going to take ill, puke in his car, call me, and I'm going to pick her up."

"What? Is she going to stick her fingers down her throat?

Man, you guys are tough."

"No, she's going to pretend to take a mint or something and pop a trilosintaxitol."

"Try to do what and where?" I asked.

"She's going to drop a trilo. They make you puke instantly. Doctors and nurses sometimes use them if a kid swallows something he shouldn't have. Failing that, they pump the stomach, I guess. Problem nowadays is they're easy to come by."

"Who the hell would want...ah, don't tell me, supermodels?"

"Supermodels, regular models, teen age bulimics, you name it."

"Man, your country is a mess. So, Tami's going to do this? You guys have gone way beyond the call of duty for me."

"And don't you forget it," Kat said with a grin.

"Um-hm. Well listen, Sonny lives in the valley so let's head down Santa Monica toward La Brea. He'll probably head north. It'll take us closer to Tami when she calls. I'll follow you."

"Anywhere?" she flirted. Clearly she was enjoying this cloak and dagger stuff too.

Kat's Dodge Ram roared to life with a deep rumble. I loved that sound. She backed up quickly and swung the truck around so she was beside me, tires squealing to a halt. Show off. Her passenger side window came down.

"What's wrong with this picture... Me with a big empty truck and you with a Pinto chock full of drums?"

"You little brat, this is classic 1965 family muscle car. Do you know that when they built this car—"

"Try to keep up, Mister Family Muscle. Tami just called." She held up a glowing cell phone. "La Brea and Third, you were right."

Kat had really put the pedal to the metal. When I pulled in behind them they were both in the truck with Sonny nowhere to be found. I shut the ol' gal down and went to Tami's window.

"Hiya doll, how you holdin' up?" I asked.

"Fine Lou," she said, chewing on what I guessed was a Tic Tac.

"Tami, Kat, thank you both so much. Tami, you really dropped a trilo as the kids say? Did it hurt?"

"It doesn't hurt. I'd sure love to brush my teeth though."

"Sonny was smitten with you girl; how did the break-up go?"

"Well, even though I upchucked in his ride, he still wanted a piece of this, if you know what I mean. So, when he tried to stop me from getting out, he might have met with a shot to the solar plexus."

"He might have, might he?" I smiled.

I grinned the whole way home. I had reason to. I was about to make out like a world-class hero to a beautiful woman who was winning my love. I couldn't wait to call her with the news. First, though, this hero needed a sandwich.

I had just enough sliced turkey and cheese left to make my world-famous 'School's Out Grilled Turkey-Cheese Sandy. It got its name because when I graduated from The Percussion House I made this sandwich for a very cute Swedish jazz drummer named Pricilla. She liked it so much that she showed her appreciation to this budding drummer for ninety minutes—then we got cleaned up and attended our grad banquet.

With ingredients on the counter, I hauled a Japanese beer out of the fridge and took a man-sized pull. It was now possible to start building. I popped two slices of twelve grain into the toaster and checked the time. The key here is forty-five seconds on level four, on a seven-level toaster, tops.

A healthy dollop of butter slid around the skillet on low heat. I brought the toast to a plate and buttered all sides. Down went the turkey on one side. For spices I added cracked black pepper, a touch of cayenne, and the same amount of smoked rock sea salt. Before continuing, I killed the rest of the beer and hauled another from the fridge.

Next the cheeses, yes cheeses, went on top of the turkey. Brie and smoked gouda. Onto these guys went another two cranks from the black pepper grinder. My excitement was building as I increased the heat under the pan. I added the pre-buttered twelve-grain roof and depressed lightly before moving it all to the pan. The real cooking was to begin so another pull from the beer was required. The process is precise and cannot be messed with.

As the cheeses began to melt, I peeked beneath the bread and noticed the bread was golden brown. I flipped it with a violin maker's care. The butter splashed, but it was okay, because I had my signature apron on that reads: Drummer's Cook with Rhythm.

More cheese escaped the sandwich and dribbled out the side. Another peek with the spatula and "School's Out" was ready. With the full sandwich and two-thirds-full beer, I headed to my couch. The melted cheeses, warm turkey and heat from the spices, oh baby, I was rocking and rolling.

I hauled out my phone and sent a group text to Kat, Tami and Jake, thanking them. I sent along a picture of the sandwich and beer. Kat and Tami responded with happy face emojis and other emoji images I couldn't understand. It was intentional, because they know I can't stand emojis and never use them— ever.

Jake called instead of texting.

"So what's next?"

"After I finish this world-class sandwich and a few more pops, I'll hit the rack and call Angela in the morning. I'm also going to get with the ladies tomorrow and figure out the drop."

"Anything else?"

"Yeah, the night we grabbed the gear one of the trucks was full, so I left a message with the cops. But, truth be told, I have no idea if the cops knew the equipment was stolen."

"We'll head to the station tomorrow. I'll walk you through it."

"Why can't I go on my own? Is it because you're a cop? Were a cop?"

"You want me to save you time or not?"

"Count me in."

After clicking off with Jake I turned up the sound on the television. The news showed another victim to "spiked" cocaine. This time it was a young black kid, male, that couldn't have been sixteen years old. It was a familiar news scene: neighbors outside on the street, weeping mother held up by a sibling to the deceased.

I've never been a fan of coke, and not for any moral high-ground position, but rather because I've seen more musical talent pissed away at the hands of the fluffy white powder than I care to remember.

My phone buzzed. I imagined it was Kat and Tami firing more emojis my way, but it was Michael Carruthers informing me that we were 'back on line.' He asked if I could open up for a hip-hop band at ten a.m. Michael had to be desperate for cash to pay for his new prized security door because I've never met a hip-hopper in my life up for a ten o'clock rehearsal. Still, I texted him back, saying that I was up for the task.

I killed my beer, rinsed my dishes then hit the rack. This drummer was beat.

I enjoyed a blissful two hours' sleep until my phone woke me at six a.m.

"Lou Crasher? This is Rex Spivey, sorry about the hour."

"It's not the hour's fault. Who did you say you were?"

"Rex Spivey."

"Is this the real Rex Spivey, or a knockoff?"

"I was told you're a funny guy."

I had half a glass of water on my nightstand. It tipped over as I reached for my bedside lamp. I could hear the drip, drip sound as Spivey asked if everything was okay.

"I'm good. I was just working out and dropped the dumb-bells...pushing too much weight, I suppose."

"You always work out at this hour?"

"I've been working out non-stop since 2006, when James Brown died."

"I see... Pretty quick with the lines you are, Crasher. I got your number from Stacy Krunch from the Percussion House.

She said you two are friends."

"We are. What can I do for you?" I asked, picking up the glass and smacking my head on the lampshade on the way up.

"Well, I've got a little matter that needs looking into."

It was time to throw the covers back and sit up. Rex Spivey was lead percussionist for the Los Angeles Philharmonic for close to fifteen years. I hadn't heard of him then. But, after his symphonic career, he made headlines as a hot shot music producer. He launched artists from pop divas to country starlets, to a handful of heavy metal heads in between. I could not begin to imagine what he'd want with me at six in the morning.

I started pacing. I hear things better on the move.

"I'm listening Mr. Spivey."

"Do you mind listening in person? It's a sensitive topic best left off the airwaves."

"Sure, I'll buzz you up."

"Ha, no I'm actually at home in my Beverly Hills house."

"I know, I was crackin'-wise," I said.

"Stacy said you were funny."

"Do you want me to come out now?"

"Oh no—I just pulled an all-nighter. I need to hit the sack."

"I got a shift today until six, how's seven?"

"That'll work fine. If you don't want to valet, just park between the Bentleys and tell the guys I said it was okay."

"That's all it'll take? No code word or secret handshake?"

"No, that's it. Say, before you go, Stacy mentioned you're a guy that knows the importance of discretion. I hope she's right about that."

"Majored in it."

"See you at seven."

Since I was up pacing, I thought it pointless to go back to bed. Furthermore, I was going to meet Jake at seven-thirty. Angela would have to wait a little longer for the happy news, but that was okay since the processor was safe and sound. I threw my sweats on and ventured to my little park. By seven-fifteen I was at the Van Nuys police station walking across the parking lot to the building. Jake was out front.

I held one side of the double glass doors for Jake. If this were a dentist's office, the few people not transfixed by cell phones would give us a glance before getting back to Pokémon or chatting with friends. In a cop shop, two brothers walking in gains all eyeballs. The eyeballs lock and hold until the two brothers make their intentions known. Once it was plain that we wanted the stolen property desk, everyone's body language relaxed.

The thick-necked cop—with fingers to match his neck—had the suspicious eyes of a regular cop and the bored eyes of a stolen property cop. I was tempted to snap my fingers in front of his face to make sure he was awake. Jake stood like a piece of furniture and stared at the officer. I did the talking.

"We're here to report stolen property. Actually, I'm here to report the location of stolen property."

With a sigh, the cop struggled to reach behind him and retrieve a standard form.

"Say, why don't you keep those in a handier spot? Like that tray to your left?"

"That tray's got another purpose. Here, fill this out and—"

The double glass doors opened with a loud thud. We turned to see six officers, each escorting prisoners. One cop with the name-tag 'Cooper,' had two prisoners; one was handcuffed and one was in zip ties. Five of the guys were small and wiry, like feisty little dogs. One huge bald guy had a massive silverback gorilla tattooed on his skull. Underneath the animal, the tatoo read: *No one gets out alive...kill them all.*

He was the big dog, and for some crazy reason Cooper had him in the ties while the cuffs were on the smaller man. The big dog turned his body and pinned Cooper to the wall.

"Listen to me, Officer Cooper, I'm gonna break your back in three places and then I'm gonna visit your wife."

SNAP! The big dog broke out of his zip ties and made a move for Cooper's gun. Our stolen property guy struggled out of his chair and came around the desk to help his brother in blue.

A prisoner that was already in the lobby, cuffed to a bench, repeatedly called for the newcomers to "kill these fuckin' pigs." Jake and I held our spots. I was ready to duck for cover in the event the prisoner got hold of the gun. Which is exactly what happened.

It was pandemonium and difficult to see exactly who was winning. POW! A bullet tore into the floor tile, narrowly missing the cop's foot. Stolen Property Cop managed a good shot to the big guy's head with his billy club but then took an elbow to the face for it. Jake stood up.

"Let's go, Lou."

"Now?"

Jake didn't answer as he headed toward the door. To get out the door we had to get past the fray. I followed behind, hands at the ready. The brawl was brutal. Heads were butted and clobbered. Cops took kicks to groins and shins, somebody got maced and the gun went off a second time as Jake and I squeezed past the brawl. By the time we reached the door, the cops had the upper hand. Reinforcements from the parking lot sprinted toward the front door.

I kept checking over my shoulder as we walked to our rides. Jake never looked back.

"That felt weird doing nothing, Jake."

"What side would you have chosen?"

"I'm not on either one of those sides. Are you kidding me?"

"Which is why we left. They'll be forever processing those guys after this."

"Meaning they'd never get to a brother and his truck-full-of-gear issue."

"You're learning, Junior," he said, climbing onto his motorcycle. He fired it up and left.

I tried to call Angela again but got routed to voicemail.

Again. Things looked a bit calmer inside the cop shop, but without Jake for backup, I decided to chill another bit before trying to blow the whistle on Abbott.

I hopped into the ol' gal and pointed her toward Hollywood. I'd be early for my shift, which was okay by me. It would give me time to get behind the drums and try and understand what the hell just happened.

The Practice Joint was already open when I arrived. Two voices came from the office. The bald-tires-peeling-out-on-gravel voice I recognized as Gladys's. The male voice was unfamiliar.

"Well lookie here, it's Handsome Lou. How they hangin' pissant?"

"None of your business, Gladys."

"This is Carlos, but I call him Carlito as in *Carlito's Way*, because he has his way with me." She cackled until a short cough erupted.

"Lou Crasher, nice to meet you."

Carlos was six months shy of his twenty-sixth birthday. Latino, well built, and looked like he walked off the set of a *telenovella* show.

"What are you two doing here?"

"My brother says he hasn't heard from you in a while, so I told him I'd swing by and see how you were…make sure you weren't hangin' out with some fairies, doing god knows what in here."

"Your dementia's getting worse, Gladdy-baby. Carlos, are you sure you know what you're doing with—" I asked pointing a thumb Gladys's direction.

"Si senior, Gladys is, how you say, dreamy."

Gladys rocked back laughing while I shook my head. Carlos could be a model, hell, a supermodel with the right agent, but here he was all hunked-out and drooling over a smart-mouthed, boozin' seventy-two-year-old.

"Well I'm going to call Eddie later and bring him up to speed. I found all of the stolen gear, by the way."

"Whoopie ding dong doo, Louis," she said, pulling a cigarette out of her pack and holding it for Carlos to light.

Say, big Eddie seems fond of you, Lou. Can't say why. Michael been acting screwy lately?"

"Kinda, why?"

"Well, probably because his daddy's got a new son." She paused. "And a black one at that."

"Carlos, you know this woman is a racist, right?"

"Si, but the *corazón* wants what the *corazón* wants, señor."

And with that comment, I threw them both out of the office. With my limited sleep, I decided to put my feet up where Gladys's red cowboy boots had rested and catch forty winks. Ten o'clock came and went with no sign of the hip-hop group. Ten-thirty and ten fifty-five also came and went.

I did a quick trip to all of the rooms, wanting to check on the workmen's handywork. The rooms weren't good as new, but better than pre-breakin. The work phone rang as I returned to the office.

"Big Eddie Carruthers, I was just going to call you and bring you up to speed."

"Well would ya look at that, we're on the same page, then. Before I forget, did my son tell you that the hip-hop band canceled?"

"No, but being that it's eleven I surmised."

"Cripes, what's wrong with that son of mine? I passed the message on to him and told him—"

Evie interrupted from the background, telling Eddie to go easy on the boy—mothers and their sons.

"Easy? That boy is a forty-two-year-old man Evie, now stop buttin' in. I'm talkin' to the whiz kid for heaven's sake. Lou, are ya still there? I wouldn't blame ya if you're not?"

"Yeah, I'm here Eddie."

As I updated Eddie about finding Angela's gear he congratulated me and called me a whiz kid close to fourteen more times. Evie piped up near the end of the conversation and suggested that Eddie and I get an apartment together.

The rest of the day was fairly slow. Most of the regulars didn't know we were back in business. Apparently Michael forgot to notify more than half of them so that's what I did in between bands and catnaps. Most of the groups were glad to hear from me, as our joint is one of the cheapest in town and we have no rules about how much booze and pot they consume on the premises.

Ten minutes before closing Michael showed up looking more sleep-deprived than me, with a topping of skittish.

"Have you talked to my dad today?"

"Yeah, this morning."

"The hip-hop band called—"

"I figured it out when they didn't show. Brothers and sisters in hip-hop don't do anything before noon."

"Well yeah, but these guys sounded different, okay?"

"Okay."

"Look I just came by for the cash." He sounded defensive.

"Sure. Everything all right boss?"

"Why does everyone keep asking me that? Is everything all right with you?"

"Well, I had a kitten as a little boy and sometimes I miss him, but other than that I'm all right."

"Don't be a smart ass, Lou, I'm your boss."

"Come on, Mike, lighten up. I'm just playing."

"If you wanna play something, go play your drums," he said, storming out.

If I had been playing my drums, he might have found a drumstick lodged in his eye.

I took care of the garbage, turned off the P.A. systems, checked the bathrooms then locked the place up. I'd have loved to be headed to Angela's to spend the next three days there—curtains closed, phones off, fridge full of necessities—and rock 'n' roll between the sheets, but I was heading to Rex Spivey's, the famed star-maker who needed me for something.

During our call he'd mentioned pulling an all-nighter, which for a guy like him, could have been as innocent as a late-night recording session. Or, if rumors were legit, it meant cocaine, hookers, a jam session and perhaps a circus animal or two.

I was tired to the point of punchy but I was Beverly Hills-bound. The deeper the ol' gal and I crept into the Hills, the wider the streets got, the finer the cars, and the bigger the houses. The ol' gal and I felt as though we were crashing a party.

The drive had high-buck pavers with immaculately manicured tufts of lawn sprouting between the stones. I pulled up past a large fountain with what I'd guess was a Greek god spewing water from his trident and penis. Three valet parkers wore the expected expressions any valet parkers would when working in a sea of Teslas, Lambourginis, Porches, Jaguars and Bentleys, when a '65 Mustang in need of a paint job pulls up.

"Sorry Bud, but this is a private party," the ringleader smirked.

"I'm the entertainment. I'm supposed to strip down and jump out of a cake. I'll park between the Bentleys. Toodle-oo."

I didn't wait for his response, which forced him to jog behind my ride. I put her in park and got out.

"What the fuck do you think you're doing? Get this piece o' shit outta here."

"I'm with Valet Parkers of America and this is a routine inspection. Do you realize you've broken three codes already?"

A man Mick Jagger-skinny with sunglasses atop his bleached-blond tips came out in lavender-colored silk pants and a cobalt blue Japanese Kimono. He was shirtless and had a booming laugh out of the side of his mouth that didn't have the thick Cuban cigar in it.

"Steven, Steven, it's okay. I told him to park there. Welcome," he said, shaking my hand. "Any trouble finding the place? Good, come on in," he said, not waiting for my answer.

The place was busy with people. Turns out I was crashing a party after all. Most had the entertainment industry look but a good handful looked like politicians, some local, some Washington. If Spivey had pulled an all-nighter he showed no signs. He put an arm around me and walked me past the scowling valets and into the mix of his giant pool party.

"Welcome to paradise, Mr. Crasher," he said, spreading a hand wide.

I'd seen this scene a thousand times, only it was in movies. It appeared as though the one percent lived in accordance with the rumors. The party was in full effect. Buff dudes and knock-out dames in bikinis floated by, or lazed in the pool. A D.J. had set up shop adjacent to a large outdoor kitchen. Being a live player of an actual instrument, I'm not a fan of D.J.s but, to this bald woman's credit, she was playing The Big Payback by James Brown. We made eye contact. I tipped my imaginary hat. She nodded back.

"That's the godfather of soul, right Lou?"

"You bet."

Across the pool in a large grassy area was a man dressed as a clown. He was introducing his pet Alpaca to a small group of naked women. Spivey caught my gaze.

"That's Chick, the Alpaca's name is Aura. That group of nude broads sorta follow him for lack of a better term."

He lowered his voice, "They're all tripping on peyote."

"Including the Alpaca?" I asked.

"Ha! That's good."

A woman that scored eleven out of ten in a bikini came up and kissed me on the cheek.

"Tell me this is him, Rex," she said.

"Sorry doll, he's here for something else."

"Oh pooh," she said, and stood in front of us pouting like a pre-teen.

"Tell you what, Sapphire, if my deal with Mr. Crasher goes smoothly, and he's up for it, you two can bang until my cows come home," he paused. "And I ain't got any cows, get it?" He belly-laughed. "But not until you take care of my other guy."

"That's right, grandma used to say, 'business before Crasher,'" I said.

Sapphire giggled and did a full body shimmer as if she were at the Arctic Circle wearing a flapper dress. Spivey guided me toward what looked like a pool house.

Spivey barely got his hand on the doorknob when a teen of about seventeen with a sad attempt at a goatee, decked out in designer clothes, came running up.

"Dad, I need like two hundred bucks."

"Shit, already?" As he dug into the silk pants he said, "Say hi to Mister Crasher, Tyler. Don't be a dick."

"What up?"

"What up? Back atcha, Tyler."

He gave me a look like I was strange. Spivey pulled out a wad full of hundreds, thicker than two Gideon bibles, and gave two bills to his son.

"Hey, what do you need this for anyway?"

"It's hard out here for a pimp," Tyler said, quoting a much-used line from *Hustle and Flow* starring Terence Howard. Later it became a song lyric. But I digress...

"Seriously, don't be a dick, Tyler."

"You don't be a dick, Dad," Tyler said, moving off through the crowd. He stopped and pulled two shots off the tray of a passing waitress and shouted, "I'm taking one of the Bentleys."

"Like hell you are, take the M3."

His son just downed two shots and was about to climb behind four hundred and fifty horsepower of German engineering...with two hundred bucks in his wallet. Good times. If he lives through them.

"Kids can be dicks, Mr. Crasher. I don't recommend them if you haven't got any already."

"Noted."

Rex Spivey opened both French doors simultaneously for effect and let me in. It turned out the pool house was actually a beautiful library and home theater room. Two walls had floor-to-ceiling white-painted bookcases. Not a single book had any breathing room. At the farthest corner from the doors sat a leather-top oak desk at a forty-five-degree angle. To the left was a fireplace, also framed by more books. Over the fireplace was a seventy-inch TV that could be viewed from one of four over-sized black leather theater chairs. The final wall, which took the eye back to the entry, was packed with a stack of books. The bookshelf they would call home was currently under construction.

He waved a hand theme-park-host style at the room.

"Are you impressed by all the books, etcetera?"

"Does wow cover it? When does a big-time producer have time to read all this jazz?"

"What do you know about me? Can I call you Lou?"

"Lou works. I know that by your second year with the Phil—"

"Wait, wait I'm such a dick I didn't even offer you a drink. What'll you have?"

"That's a tough one. In a room like this, with fine oak bookcases, a beautiful bubinga wood desk, and leather-bound classics, a man yearns for Macallan scotch, twenty-five years. But the pool party outside says 'margarita' with top-shelf tequila."

"You're a likable son of a bitch. How did you know that desk is bubinga?"

"Played a snare drum made from it once." I played, but never bought it, once I heard that heavy demand by American woodworking enthusiasts and instrument makers cause loggers to pillage exotic African forests for the lumber. It was a beautiful-sounding snare, however.

"Let's drink what the room suggests, huh? Got your Macallan right here," he said, grabbing his crotch and laughing a high pitch laugh. The cigar nearly fell out of his mouth.

After the laugh subsided, he pulled a bottle from a tiny makeshift bar. He poured. We clinked and took sips.

"So you were saying."

"I happen to know that by your second year with the Phil, you began writing the parts for the percussion section and then eventually the whole orchestra."

"Fuck that, who cares? What about my creations? My artists? I've made stars from country rock to heavy metal and back."

"Really? I hadn't heard."

"What? Oh, you're fucking with me." He smiled, pointing the stogie at me.

"Mr. Spivey, I gotta jam to the point. What can I do for you?"

"Right to business. After I spoke to Stacy, I googled you. There wasn't much, so I called her back and picked her brain."

He downed his scotch and poured himself another. I held at the one in my hand.

"This may sound racist, but you've obviously heard of Fredrick Douglass, right?"

"Yes, and it wouldn't have sounded racist if you just asked the question without the 'this may sound' jazz, but go on."

"Shit, sorry. There's an old colonial snare drum that is connected to Frederick Douglass..." He stopped talking and stared hard at me.

"And?"

"And that drum was stolen," he paused and held his tumbler close to his mouth, "from this very house. It was my drum. I want it back, and I want you to find it."

I took a short pull and sat down. A colonial-age snare drum was amazing on its own because the snare drum and drummers had a massive hand in building these United States.

"Do you know anything about the drummers of that era, Lou?"

"I know that the colonial snare drummer was the rock star of his day. He was treated on par with an officer, if not better."

"And why do you think that was?"

"The military snare drummer used various rudiments, strung them together into cadences, if you will, and moved troops around the battlefield. That, my friend, is one valuable cat. I read somewhere, I can't remember where, that platoons would often go on missions with the intent to capture the drummer.

He'd turn out to be a big bargaining chip during hostage negotiations."

"And not only that, Lou, they were well treated when captured; comfortable lodgings, gourmet meals, and given fine-ass women, too."

Either the scotch or the subject matter had us both amped up. Spivey got up and topped my drink off.

"You're out of fuel, Lou, and ya can't fly without fuel."

"Thanks."

"Cigar?"

"No thanks." I got up and checked out his book collection as I continued.

"Imagine your unit is trying to take a hill but every time you make a move or plan a sneak attack, the other side reacts and thwarts you every time. Sure, the word comes down from generals and field commanders, but the guy that really makes the machine do what it's supposed to is the guy that plays a secret drum line not unlike Morse code—the drummer, baby. Can I get an amen?"

"A-fuckin'-men."

"And let us not forget that this cat marched onto the battlefield without a gun. Talk about a stud!"

"Goddamn it, you're a likable son of a bitch, Lou."

I picked up Homer's *The Illiad*. "I dug this. Never finished it though. Forgot it on the back of a tour bus."

"Take it, it's yours. *The Odyssey* too."

"That's all right, I'm cool," I said, sitting down.

"Mr. Spivey, lack o' sleep and fine scotch has me dizzy like a teenage diva. You said something about Frederick Douglass. Lay that news on me, brother."

Spivey got up from his chair and stood over me with excitement in his eyes. Up close I could see how he'd pulled an all-nighter and appeared daisy-fresh: cocaine. The pinwheel pupils, slight chatter to the teeth, and the sweaty brow and upper lip in an air-conditioned room said it all.

"Get this, there was a drummer like the type you're talking

about. He's fighting for the Confederates, okay? So, the war ends and he feels like crap for all the death he's caused. He's conflicted, you see, because his daddy was a military man and all that. But this guy has a liberal heart, do you follow?"

"So far."

"Good. Now around this time he starts hearing about a free slave, Mr. Douglass, and he likes the scuttlebutt on what the man's been preaching about the abolitionist movement and all that up in New York. So what does he do? He hugs his daddy good-bye and leaves Maryland bound for the Big Apple. He wants to meet the man in person. Isn't it wild?"

"You've got my attention, keep going."

"Right. So he gets there and is granted an audience with Douglass. This dude is literally floored by him. He's so moved by Douglass's magnitude that, well, guess what he does?"

I took a slow sip of the scotch and let it sit on my tongue a moment. "He gifts Frederick Douglass with his personal snare drum," I said.

"You bet your sweet ass he did," Spivey said, clinking my glass.

"And this drum ended up in your hands? Shit stew on a soda cracker."

"I searched for that drum ten years before getting my paws on it. She sat in my office on the other side of the house. But two days ago it was stolen."

"And that's why I'm here."

"Yes, sir. Do you want me to show you where I kept it, or how does this work?"

"Quick question. Other than Stacy's endorsement, why me? Why not use your insurance company?"

He finally left his standing position, giving me space, and moved along one of the book walls, touching each book with an index finger as he walked.

"Simple truth is, I don't—or didn't, rather—officially own the drum," he said, using air quotes around the word "own."

"But I've got a buyer that'll give me eighty cents on the dollar, compared to what it would get at a Sotheby's auction."

"I see...and you don't want to tarnish your reputation or go to jail for a high-buck drum. A green-eyed journeyman drummer with a sunny disposition is the perfect sap to steal your stolen dingus for you. That about right?"

"Pre-fucking-cisely," he said topping off our Macallans. "Did I mention the twenty-five K I'll pay you?"

CHAPTER 18

I'd missed a call from Angela while I was at Spivey's mansion-crib. So, I couldn't resist swinging by her place to present her with the processor in person. But there was no answer at the buzzer and my call went to voicemail. I left a semi-smooth message and drove home. By the time I walked through my door exhaustion was setting in, but I wanted to get onto this Spivey jazz while it was fresh. Twenty-five thousand dollars will do that to a journeyman drummer. I called Stacy Krunch to double-check her vouching for me, which I knew she had, and to see what she knew about Spivey.

"Hiya doll, it's Lou Crasher."

"So my caller I.D. is accurate then. You calling about Spivey?"

"I am at that. Thanks for the endorsement by the way but same question I asked Spivey, why me?"

"Word on the street and this school for that matter is you're a drummer that can find things. Good work, Lou.

"Why thank you, but dang, news travels fast."

"It expands too. Is it true you smashed Abbott's car window then beat the crap out of him?"

"Is that what the street word is? Expands is right. I haven't even taken him down yet and don't know if I will."

"Please do. Spivey was my way of paying you for taking out

the Abbott trash."

"You got a history with Abbott or something?"

"Tangentially, but that's another story for another time, brother."

She'd shut the door on Abbott so I worked Spivey.

"What do you know about Rex Spivey?"

"Just what the papers used to say when he first made a name for himself. He parties hard, has the Midas touch with artists and has a ton o' dough. Can you tell me what he wants you to find?"

"I should probably sit on it."

"You're right, you should. I just wanted to see if you'd spill because I'm a beautiful woman."

"Oh you're beautiful enough but I still ain't spillin'."

"I also know he's into kinky sex and loves blow, so don't get caught up in that life, Lou. Just find his bauble, take whatever pay he gives you and move on."

"You ever have any dealings with Rex? Ever met him?"

"No, never. Saw him play with the Phil a few times but that's it."

"They say he was good."

"He was. Say Lou, you ever think about doing the sleuthing thing full time?"

"No not really, I—"

"You just wanted the girl—I get it. Men have no imagination."

"Anything else on Spivey?" I sighed.

"He's got a kid living with him. Spoiled brat—got two DUIs."

"He was on his way to a third when I met him."

"Well, that's all I've got handsome."

"That's a lot, thanks, and thanks for the hookup."

"Girlfriend or not, you're taking me to dinner when all of this is done."

"I thought you'd never ask."

"I didn't ask. I told."

She clicked off.

***

I barely finished my beer nightcap, which is saying something. The next morning I bypassed my park workout and did ab exercises to Deep Purple's *Machine Head* album. As I waited for my coffee to brew I anticipated my reunion with Angela. I pictured her big smile, a big hug and then moving east through her apartment to the bedroom for a "thank you, Crasher" rock n roll beneath the sheets.

My vision didn't come to be; I got her voicemail, again. Next, I called Kat and left another voicemail saying I was trying to track down Angela for the drop and wanted to know when I could pick up the gear.

Nowadays the cellphone is in everybody's hand, their pocket or purse, or within reach ninety-eight per cent of the day—yet nobody's ready with the pickup when Crasher calls: these times they are-a-silly.

I drained the coffee and worked down a bowl of cereal before hitting the shower. As the hot water beat down I thought back to Nigel Brixton, the English bloke from the Woodland Hills rehearsal space. Dollars to drums, Brixton would have skinny on Rex Spivey.

"Nigel," I said aloud, toweling off, "I'm coming to see you, chap."

I could easily have called, but I like to look at a fella's facial moves and body language during a dialogue session. Besides, you can't rush a brother off the phone when he's right in your mug.

An electronic chime went off as I entered the shop. Nigel was behind the counter. He didn't pull his eyes from his seventeen-inch computer screen.

"The chime is new," I said. "Driving you insane yet?"

Without raising his head he peered over his split lenses.

"Ah, Mister...Crasher, I think it is, yes? Indeed, the pearly tones are the owner's latest security measure," he said, adding an eyeroll. He pulled off the glasses.

"So what brings you in today, young man?"

"Do you remember a cat by the name of Rex Spivey, the L.A. Philharmonic percussionist?"

"Yes, and now he turns talentless twits into pop stars."

"Yeah, that Spivey. Know anything about him or your paths ever cross?"

"Oh yes, after his time with the Phil there was a window—prior to working with the talentless—when he rehearsed here with an impressive jazz trio."

"He played kit then?"

"Bloody good, too. I didn't approve of the hangers-on, mind you, what with the partying and all that, but they were bloody great musicians."

"Anything else?"

"He spent lavishly. Rumor has it he has a thing for—" Nigel touched his left nostril with an index finger.

"Likes the powder, does he?"

"Shh man, I'm trying to run a bloody business here. I shouldn't be discussing clientele past or present."

And with that Nigel clammed up.

I climbed back into the 'stang and headed to my place of business. The Practice Joint was back online. The robbery erased from the minds of rockers, players moved on. Angela's band was yet to schedule rehearsal time. It didn't add up. I had her gear and still hadn't heard from her. My feelings for her aside, this didn't make sense from her band's standpoint. Musicians need instruments, plain and simple, and some even value their axe or drums more than their spouses or girlfriends. Angela also mentioned her band was due in the studio, so why not call on the guy with the gear? I didn't like it.

My shift was uneventful other than a Bob Dylan cover band in room E. They needed a mop as the bass player had tipped a bong over, and apparently the guys couldn't stand the smell of the bong water. I arrived with a mop to find that the water had soaked into the worn-out carpet, not the short section of dated lino. I wheeled bucket and mop back to the office.

"What the hell, man, we can't jam like this," the bandleader protested. "The smell's bad for my vocal chords."

I ignored him and returned with a spray bottle, doused the spot, and left. Their faces said they weren't satisfied, but they voiced nothing as my face said that was all the customer service The Joint had to offer on that day.

An hour later I was locking the place up. My phone buzzed twice as I was securing the new steel gate. I let it go to voicemail. Back in the ol' gal I revved her up and let her idle as I checked my messages. The first call was from Eddie Carruthers. He sounded upbeat.

"When ya coming by to visit the ol' lady and me?"

I called him back and told him I was on my way over. The second message was from Dave Abbott, offering me a gig at the Hollywood Lingerie club. My ruse with Abbott was still holding. I knew the club. It's set up to appear like a unisex strip club with exotic dancers but is actually a live rock 'n' roll bar. The female servers wear bustiers a half size too small while the male bartenders don a Chippendales-style bow tie number. One might call the attire gimmicky, tacky and over the top. Still, I texted back that I'd do the gig. I put my 'stang in gear and rolled out.

Inside a rental car on Lilac Street, Dave Abbott watched and waited for a classic red Mustang to pass down the busy thoroughfare of Highland Avenue. In retrospect, it seemed a little too convenient that Crasher had shown up at Candy's door looking for a job. When the red classic flashed by, Abbott pulled up to the stop sign at Highland, then folded into traffic four cars back. He wanted a closer look at this drummer.

Across from the Knickerbocker Apartments, Crasher pulled

up, so Dave parked half a block down and tailed him on foot, on the opposite side of the street. As Lou approached the intercom for the apartments and busied himself at the panel, Abbott crossed the street and ducked behind a black Mercedes AMG G35. Abbott crouched low and moved to the edge of the building, at the foot of the steps, and hauled out his cell phone.

Crasher was waiting for his party to answer, so Abbott took the opportunity to snap away on his phone. A moment later Crasher announced himself and was let into the lobby. Abbott shielded the sun from his screen and checked the pics. He zoomed in on the best picture and was able to see the name and apartment number.

Vaulting over the low-rise steps, he peeked into the lobby. Crasher was waiting in front of the elevator. Once Lou climbed aboard, Abbott buzzed the apartment number into the intercom.

"Hello? Lou?" It was the voice of some old timer. Abbott stayed silent, hoping the party in apartment twelve-eleven would re-buzz, thinking Crasher hadn't gotten the door in time.

"Damn buzzer's on the fritz again, Evie," he heard the old timer grumble. The keypad chirped and the door clicked open.

Fuckin' A! Abbott let himself into the lobby. He found the staircase and hightailed it to the seventh floor. Creeping down the hall like a nervous cat, he reached the apartment door. It was made of cheap pressboard, and sound floated through it like tissue paper.

Big Eddie Carruthers stood in the apartment foyer and beckoned me toward him with a big grin on his face.

"Aw, come on Eddie, you don't need to greet me like this," I said. "You should be on your lounger in slippered feet with a scotch at your elbow."

"Oh knock it off, kid," he said, giving me a firm handshake, followed by a stiff pat on the back.

We took our seats but I was up immediately when Evie arrived with a tray in her hands.

"Hello, Evie."

"Hello, Louis."

"Let me help you with that tray."

"Not until the day I can't do it for myself, youngster," she smiled, putting the tray on the coffee table.

"Evelyn Carruthers, not again with the milk and godforsaken cookies," Eddie barked.

"He thinks calling me by my full name means I'll listen to him," Evie said, ignoring her husband.

"Do you not see that he's a man, Evie? I mean for heaven's sake."

"Hush up, you cantankerous old goat." Then she turned to me and pointed a threatening finger.

"Louis, you enjoy your milk and cookies, do you hear me?"

"Yes Ev—, Mrs. Carruthers," I said, grabbing two cookies and a glass of milk. Evie retreated back to the kitchen.

"My apologies, Lou, but my wife thinks she's got a shot at winning hostess of the year."

"I heard that," she called.

Eddie lowered his voice to a whisper, "Louis, hand me a glass of that milk and a couple cookies, will ya, son?"

"Just give him one, Louis, he's got to watch his sugar levels."

Eddie and I exchanged shocked looks at how good Evie's hearing was. Eddie and I were quiet a moment while we dipped cookies into our glasses. Evie came back in and joined in. What a trio we were, three grownups snacking like toddlers at daycare.

"So, Lou, I hear you managed to locate the stolen gear."

"Not only locate but you retrieved it, isn't that right, Lou?" Evie added.

"Holy smokes, Lou," Eddie said, putting his empty glass on the table. "You know Lou, if we could pay you more we would. It's just we're not bringing in the dough, ya know what I mean?"

"Sure Eddie, I know."

"Can we offer you more hours? Would that help?" Evie asked.

"Thanks Evie, but I'm okay. The hours I get free me up to pursue this wondrous music career I'm building," We all chuckled at that one.

"Geez, it's a tough business, the music business, especially here in L.A. Not to mention D.J.s and computers are edging guys out like you, I'm afraid."

"You're really hip to the scene, Eddie, I'm impressed."

"Old guys rule, Lou. We know stuff."

"Oh please," Evie said.

Eddie made his eyes into slits. Evie warned that something was cooking "in that brain of his."

"You ever consider taking a stab at the P.I. business?" My phone vibrated. I ignored it and put it face down on the coffee table.

"I have to say this little gig has been more exciting than work at the Joint, no offense."

"None taken."

My phone vibrated again and rumbled across the table.

"You better take that, it may be related to your case," Evie said with a wink.

"Sorry," I said, picking it up. I walked to the tiny entry hall. "This is Lou."

"Lou Crasher?" It was a woman's voice full of business.

"Yes."

"Mr. Crasher, my name is Jaclyn Malloy. I'm a nurse here at Hollywood General. Are you a relative of Robert Coldwater?"

"Rob—you mean Bobby?"

"Yes, he gave your name as next of kin when he was brought in."

"Brought in? What happened?"

"I'm afraid he's had an excessive dose of cocaine."

"He O.D.'d? No!" I said. Evie and Eddie were out of their seats and moving slowly toward me with worried looks on their faces.

"Yes, and I'm afraid he's shown signs of using the bad strain that's been going around. I'm sure you've seen it on the news."

I covered the phone and gave the Carruthers a quick version.

"What's his condition?"

"I'm not at liberty to say too much as I'm not his physician, but I can tell you it's not good. The doctors had to, um, induce coma. I'm very sorry."

"I'm on my way."

I zigzagged through traffic like a cop with his cherry lit up and got to Hollywood General in six minutes. Interesting that Bobby referred to me as next of kin. Perhaps he thought I'd be allowed to visit him in that case, or maybe he was so out of it he thought we were family.

A female doctor of Middle Eastern descent spoke with a woman at reception. I was in luck, as she was talking about Bobby.

"Pardon my interrupting, but I'm Bobby's cousin, Lou Crasher," I lied. "How's he doing?"

"Hello, Mr. Crasher. Please, let's talk over here."

With a gentle palm on my back, she guided me around a corner to a sitting area. Bobby's girlfriend, Julie, leapt to her feet and hugged me. Her body trembled against mine as she cried. I eased her away and focused on the doctor.

"Doc, what's the skinny? I understand he's in a coma?"

"Yes, in some cases we have no choice but to apply this procedure. You see, he came in like so many others, chatting incoherently, complaining of pain all over the body. He then began convulsing—"

"It was horrible," Julie said. "I was so scared."

The doctor continued. "He went into cardiac arrest."

"His heart stopped?" I asked, feeling as though I was hearing her words from the bottom of a swimming pool.

"Yes, we managed the heart issue but now we've noticed severe swelling on the brain."

"I don't suppose you know how long—"

"No sir."

"But why? Why Bobby? He's a good person," Julie whined.

The doctor folded her arms and scowled at Julie. "The reason is cocaine. The reason is bad enough but anyone who would do this drug while poison is rampant in the music community is on a suicide mission. I'm sorry but that is my opinion. Now if you will excuse me."

"One more question, please. Any ideas where this supply might be coming from?

"It seems a lot of victims are coming in from live music clubs, jam sessions, open mics—you name it. Somehow, that community is flooding with it and people are getting poisoned. Now I really must go, I have other patients."

"Understood. Thank you doctor."

Julie leaned in and sobbed into my chest.

CHAPTER 19

As I was unlocking my car door the phone buzzed. I hauled it out of my pocket with too much vigor and dropped it on the pavement.

"Damn it."

The phone slid under my ride. I got down on hands and knees, reached under and grabbed it. It still buzzed.

"Hello," I practically barked.

"Lou? Are you all right? It's Angela."

"Hey, there you are." I tried my best not to sound rattled, but it wasn't easy.

"What's going on? You sound kinda, I don't know."

"Where have you been Angela? I've got your gear, remember?"

"Whoa, take it down a notch. Do you want to call me back later?"

I tried to slow my breathing but it was no use. I was pissed. Pissed at Abbott, pissed at Bobby for being so stupid and even a little pissed at Angela. Here I'd been running all over town for her and she goes AWOL.

"No, I'd rather not call you back. I'd like to return your stuff to you. You've got a session coming up, don't you?"

"I don't like your tone, Lou."

"Look, I've got a buddy in the hospital in a coma. Another victim of that bad blow. I realize you didn't know that, but I've been trying to return your jazz to you and the radio silence gig hasn't been cool. So, apologies if my tone is in the wrong key, baby."

"Wow. Okay then, let's get me my stuff and get you your final check, and get you on your way to your rock-n-roll life. But as an aside, the radio silence you speak of was me spending day and night at the nursing home my aunt stays at, and the reception in that part of Malibu sucks."

I felt like a first-class heel. "Is she okay?"

"She had a stroke."

I felt even worse than a heel. "Sorry to hear that. Was it bad?"

Just then, a man, mid-fifties with frosted tips, driving a Tesla, called out his window. "Hey buddy, you leaving or not?"

"Hang on," I said, opening my car door.

"Angela, can I call you back?"

"Whatever."

"What—"

The Tesla honked. "Let's go brother."

Brother? Closing my door I walked toward frosted tips. A pedestrian in her late thirties pulled her phone and began filming me. I reached the Tesla.

"Look, brother, I just want the spot. Don't make this a thing."

"Do you love this car?"

"What? Yeah I love—"

"I will take her from you, do you understand? I'll make you a guest at this hospital for six months, then drive away silently in your pretty little ride. Can ya dig it...brother?"

He rolled up his window and quietly rolled away.

"Lou, you're scaring me." It was Angela. She was still on the line.

"Shit, you're still there."

"Yes, I'm still here, and not loving this side of you."

"I'll call you back."

I was hit harder than expected by Bob's coma situation. I couldn't concentrate on anything else, so I decided to stay in and take it easy before calling Angela back. I ran through Abbott's tunes a few times with my old-school CD player and rubber surfaced practice pad. There was no need to sit behind the full kit because the tunes were still locked.

I put a sandwich together on automatic pilot. I barely remember the ingredients; still, it was magnificent, thanks to muscle memory.

Next, I called the law to finish what Jake and I had attempted to do in person. It was time they popped Abbott and returned the gear to rightful owners. But I got nowhere fast other than an empty promise that someone from robbery would call me back.

I fired up the computer and checked Google to see if there was anything more to learn about Rex Spivey. It seemed the bulk of the information was about the stars he'd made. I recognized all the names but could barely name one song from each artist. I might've done it if a gun were to my head—maybe.

Next, I looked into vintage snare drums from the colonial era. There were more floating around out there than I expected. As I was reading up on drum number three, Rex Spivey called.

"Ya busy?"

"All depends. What's going on?"

"There's been a development," he paused. I heard a short, sharp sniffling sound. "I need to see you. Could you swing by?"

Could I? Would I? All I wanted was a beer and some rest. I wanted to tell Rex Spivey and the whole world to go to hell. I also wanted to make money. So I took a deep breath and said, "Grabbing my keys now."

When I got to Spivey's the party was still going. Either that, or a new party was in full swing. Outside, in the circular stone paver driveway, four giant peacocks had two valet parkers backed against a wall. A few partygoers filmed the spectacle with phones. These days the hunt to create viral videos rules. I parked in my usual spot. One of the peacocks, convinced the valet parkers were securely pinned down, turned on the onlookers and chased them into the house.

As I approached, the bird turned and shrieked at me.

"Take it easy, pal; I don't actually belong here."

The animal seemed satisfied and rejoined the other bird harassing the parkers.

The door was ajar so I let myself in. This party had a theme. Each guest had a hand-held eye mask to his face. Being mask-less I drew many stares. This had that creepy "eyes wide shut" vibe that I can't stand. A woman in a sheer black form-fitting dress handed me a mask. I wanted to refuse but remembered the twenty-five thousand Spivey was paying me.

"Thanks doll, have you seen Spivey around?"

"Spivey," she said.

"Yes, Rex Spivey, have you seen him?"

"Spivey," she giggled then skipped through the crowd like a preschooler. Her quick pace didn't suggest I follow, so I moved through the throng and searched for my client. My mask had cat-shaped eyes bedazzled with a thousand different colored stones.

A shirtless skinny dude in a grass skirt approached me on a Segway. Tethered to his wrist was a leash, and at the end of that was a live miniature pig. His mask was flat black. He parked in front of me.

"I'm Batman," he said.

"So this must be Robin," I said, bending to pet the animal.

"Finally—someone who gets me," he said excitedly.

"Where's his mask, Batman?"

"I rigged up a sweet number with elastic, but he keeps ripping it off. Don't you Robin?" he scolded.

Got any suggestions how I can get him to wear it?"

"I'm no pig whisperer but I'd bet Robin can fight crime without a mask."

"Nice."

"You seen Spivey around?"

"He's around here somewhere."

"Cool, I'll look there then."

Robin came closer and rubbed his body against my leg like a cat.

"Holy shit, he likes you. He usually hates dudes. Loves the ladies though."

"Takes a player to know a player," I said.

"Nice," he repeated, spun the Segway a hundred and eighty degrees and rolled away.

The woman who gave me my mask came back and said "Spivey" again and skipped away. I decided to take a different route from my previous visit. "Private eyes should poke around" was my understanding from Rockford and Magnum, so I obliged. Off the main great room to my left was a short hallway. I took it and ended up in a large media room with eighteen-foot-high ceilings. The place was packed, each person holding their mask in one hand and martini in the other.

Like the poolroom I'd been in before, this place had several book cases. Tucked in every six feet or so were flat screens, fourteen in all. None had sound, all were muted. Each screen had a different live concert video playing. Spivey played everything from The L.A. Philharmonic to Led Zeppelin and over to Miles Davis. People milled as if in a museum.

I felt a hand on my shoulder. I turned to find a heavyset woman with perfect teeth in a happy round face.

"Cadillac Martini."

Her smile was infectious. "Sounds like a good place to start," I said, taking the drink. "Thank you."

We clinked glasses with a cheer.

"Lou Crasher."

"Lyla."

"Pleasure is mine, Lyla."

"So what do you do, and who do you know?"

"Right to it, huh? I play drums and I've known Rex for close to forty-eight hours now, give or take. You?"

"I work in intelligence."

"I knew you were smarter than me the minute I saw you."

"Oh, a sense of humor to go with those pretty eyes."

"So are you here for fun or are you running an Op?"

"An Op? For a drummer you sure sound like you're in the movie business."

"Wait a minute, how can you tell I have pretty eyes when I'm wearing this ridiculous mask?"

"It's got eye holes dummy," she laughed.

"Harassing my guests, Lyla?" Spivey said sliding up to us. They lowered masks and air kissed cheek to cheek—a ritual I've always found peculiarly useless.

"You two getting acquainted?"

"We have. Lou's been trying to figure out the Op I'm running."

"Already figured it out," I said.

"Oh?" Spivey asked.

"It's called Operation Cadillac Martini—none of us are getting out alive."

That got me a medium-sized laugh. "Will you excuse us, Ly'?"

"Only if you bring him back when you're done."

Lyla moved to a screen showing Jimi Hendrix live at Woodstock. I lowered my mask and downed the rest of my martini.

"Good martini, huh, Crasher? My guy Axel really knows his drinks."

"Goes down like butter. Have you got anything lighter? Like a beer maybe? A brother rolling around in a classic ride in this neighborhood with a martini buzz is likely to land me in a cell."

"I get it. Follow me, and put your mask back up."

"Must I?"

"You bet your ass."

It was a slow meander through the crowd. Everyone and their dog wanted a piece of this cat. I received several "who the hell is that guy getting all of Spivey's attention" looks and welcomed them all with polite smiles.

Rex was a magnet for guys with business deals they thought Rex should get in on; up and coming artists Rex has "got to hear." Others hoped to get the man in a quiet room and bump some lines. After navigating the gauntlet, Rex pulled me into a small servants' kitchen. A half-dozen staff moved like worker ants, slipping and dodging one another as they prepped food trays. A short Latino gent in a short white jacket with slicked-back hair and a skull tattoo on his neck seemed to run the show.

"Juan," Spivey called. Juan came over.

"Juan, this is Lou Crasher. He's looking for a beer. What have we got?"

"Yes, sir. Evening, Mr. Crasher." I was thrown by his Australian accent but did my best not to show it.

"We have Corona, Corona Light, Sam Adams, Stella Artois, Heineken, and Scrimshaw, which is a pilsner from North Coast Brewing. We also have five different IPAs, would you like me to list those?"

"First of all, this sounds like my Christmas list. I'm impressed guys—even more so that you don't stock piss waters: Bud, Coors and Pabst Blue Ribbon."

"Actually we do, but judging by your stature I surmised you to be a bloke who'd avoid that level of beer."

Both my eyebrows were raised. "The Scrimshaw from North Coast, are they cold?"

"Your standard refrigerator temperature is thirty-five degrees Fahrenheit. We keep the beer fridge at thirty-three."

"Your spouse is lucky to have you, Juan. I'll take the Scrimshaw."

"Coming right up."

"Rex, whatever you're paying that man, double it."

"I'll make a note of it," he chuckled. "Now the reason I called you—"

"Dad, where the fuck have you been?" asked his rattled son Tyler. His button-down shirt matched his many-pocketed cargo shorts. His flip-flops slapped loudly on the tile floor.

160

"I've been all over. It's what one does when hosting a party, son."

"Whatever. I need three bills."

"What? You're killing me, kid. Say hi to Mr. Crasher."

"S'up Crasher?"

"The S&P 500, last time I looked."

"Whatever."

"Don't be a dick, son," Spivey interjected.

Juan arrived with my beer and poured it into a frosted mug.

"Thank you kindly."

"Juan, get me a PBR, would ya?" Tyler ordered.

"I have it on good authority that you know where the fridge is, Junior," Juan said, turning back to his staff. Tyler tried to look mortified for his daddy.

"Maybe you'll try 'please' next time, son."

"Fine, then can I fucking please have three hundred bucks?"

With a heavy sigh Spivey dug out his thick wad of hundreds. I put a firm grip on Rex's wrist.

"Put the roll away, Rex," I said. Turning to the kid, I said, "You heading to the club tonight? Good side of the velvet rope, bottle service, honeys the whole nine?"

"None of your fucking business."

I ignored the remark. "Tonight, let your buddies buy the rounds instead of your dear old dad here."

"What? Those dicks won't—"

"Work it out Tyler. Your dad's ATM is closed."

"Dad, fire this dick."

"Nope," Spivey said, somewhat weakly.

Tyler moved up close to me.

"Careful who you step to, Junior," I warned.

Tyler breathed heavily then turned and left, calling us 'dicks' over his shoulder. Rex pinched the bridge of his nose and closed his eyes.

"You don't need to say it, Lou. I know I'm one of those enabling helicopter parents."

"So don't be. Ground that helicopter and turn off the taps every once in a while."

"You don't think I tried that? He just acts out and runs to his mother and then I have to deal with her—what a nightmare." He ran a hand through his hair.

"What would you do?"

"Throw him down a flight of stairs—once a month until he learns."

"You can't be serious."

"No, metaphorically maybe. Either way this really isn't my area of expertise." I sipped my beer. "Snare drums are."

"Right, let's get into it. Do you mind if we do it here? I need to be away from all that."

We pulled two bar stools up to a high-top table. Juan came back and checked on us. We told him our drinks were sufficient.

"Sir, might I ask to be the one to implement the new policy?"

"What policy?"

"I heard we're tossing your son down some stairs."

"Don't be insubordinate, Juan." Spivey was trying to conceal a smile.

"I'll be back with some mushroom canapés."

"I like that guy, Rex."

"He's the best in the business. I poached him from Aniston. He's also one hell of a trumpet player."

"What have ya got, Rex?"

"I got a weird call, which I guess you could say is a lead—creeped me out though."

"How so?"

"You know in movies when the kidnapper makes a call with one of those altered voice machines and demands the money?"

"Mm hmm."

"Well, I got that call. The asshole that stole my drum wants fifty-K." He sipped his drink. "They could have asked for more."

"They don't know the true value or they're just desperate."

"Right."

"You gonna pay?"

"No, I'm not going to friggin' pay. You're going to get my drum back for me. I'll pay you another ten-K, seeing as this ransom business ups the danger for you."

"Thirty-five K all in?"

"Yes."

"Done. And thank you," I paused. "They don't know the drum's worth but they knew you had the drum."

"Okay."

"And it's someone you know."

Spivey stared blankly. "Tyler? Not my son, do you think?"

"Maybe. Not necessarily. I'm guessing you told him the drum's value at some point."

"Yeah, he knows."

"Then he'd have asked for more don't you think?"

"Yes, no, I don't know." Spivey's shoulders drooped with the weight of his world on them.

"You need to get me a list of your family members and staff. Then you need to make a short list of everyone who knew you had—"

Spivey's phone rang with a ring tone of Eric Clapton's "Cocaine" song. He grabbed it quickly. Whomever he'd assigned the tone to was important. He turned his back and whispered into the phone—only whispering was not in his skill set. He was irritated. He ended the call by slamming it down on the high top and nearly cracking the screen. Half the staff looked up from their work.

"What's going on here? Is everyone out to fleece me?"

"Drug dealer raised his rates, huh?"

"Shit, you heard me?"

"That and your ring tone isn't too subtle."

Rex talked about wrapping things up with me at that point. He was becoming fidgety and agitated. I'd seen the dance with many musicians.

I thought about the process of elimination. Isn't that what

Sherlock Holmes talked about? Didn't my old-school television P.I. heroes begin by ruling out the obvious suspects? Spivey was missing gear. I'd found stolen gear and knew who'd stolen it. Conclusion: Spivey's drug dealer was putting the squeeze on him.

"Rex, before you run upstairs to do a rail, I need to see your phone."

"Why? What does this have to do with my drum?"

"It's a hunch, a long shot really, but it will clear somebody from my own personal list."

He slid the phone over to me. "Do I need a passcode?"

"Four sevens."

I punched the code and looked at his most recent call. I turned the screen so he could read it.

"This was your last call, your dealer?"

"Yes."

"What's his name?"

"I don't know he just goes by the letter D."

"How soon can you get me the lists I need?"

"Tomorrow night? Email it to you?"

"Since you party at night, make it tomorrow afternoon, latest. I'll see myself out."

We stood and shook. "What was all that stuff with my phone?"

"Just working a case, champ. Say, what's tomorrow night's theme?"

"Pretty mellow. Go-Go dancers, body paint, couple jugglers. Almost forgot, there's a jam session you should come through."

"Can't. I'll see myself out. By the way, if your peacocks give me any trouble I'll take 'em out and make a nice gumbo."

"That's excessive."

"Tomorrow afternoon, Rex, don't forget."

"I won't, and thanks for the help with my kid."

"They are the future."

* * *

The smiley girl who'd given me my mask met me at the door as I was about to leave.

"Spivey," she said, following it with the same annoying giggle.

I handed her my costume. "Mask," I said opening the front door.

"Wait, leaving so soon? We haven't, you know, gotten to know each other yet."

"I know you, all right. You're the high priestess of mask distribution and utterer of Spivey. Have a pleasant evening, doll."

"But you're going to miss the body paint teaser for tomorrow's party."

I was about to crack wise but noticed the two peacocks coming my way with purpose.

"Next time, peace 'n' love."

I hopped in my ride and fired her up. The peacocks protested. I gave them a friendly wave goodbye.

CHAPTER 20

It was two in the morning when I climbed my apartment steps. I let myself in, brushed the pearly whites and hit the rack. I was exhausted.

When I woke I called the hospital. There was no change with Bobby, still in a coma. Bobby's girlfriend must have been near the nurses' station and heard the call because she called me back immediately. She cried, and was pissed that I wasn't at Bobby's bedside.

When I told her I had things to do, she said, "so did Bob but he "wouldn't be able to do them," and how nice it was for me to be conscious and walking around enjoying life, etcetera. I let her rant. I barely knew her and didn't think much either way about her, except she genuinely cared for Bob—so that was a plus.

When my responses continued to dissatisfy, she called me a jerk and hung up the phone. I felt guilty not going to see Bob but convinced myself that if I brought Abbott to his knees then I'd be helping Bob. He'd be satisfied with that—if he pulled through. The doctor will do her thing on the inside and I'll do mine in the street. That was the best option, or so I told myself.

The morning and afternoon zipped by like an up-tempo Coltrane tune. It was time for my second gig with Dave Abbott and company. I had to play at least one more gig with "Joanie" to keep suspicion off me as far as the stolen processor. With luck I'd gain more info on Abbott and find a way to take him down, or maybe not. Either way this would be my Boning Joanie swansong because it was an undercover gig and I'm no undercover agent.

The drums loaded into my ride, I hopped onto the 134 Freeway headed west, then headed south on the 101 South down toward Hollywood. The 101 was a slow go because Lady Gaga was performing at the Hollywood Bowl. I don't own any of her music but I respect her highly as an artist. She's got the business sense of Madonna with far superior vocal and song-writing ability.

A traffic cop, bulging around the middle in white gloves, held up all lanes of traffic while concert-goers, most of them costumed, crossed the street. The Bowl traffic added twenty minutes to my drive. I headed east on Sunset Boulevard at a cool thirty-five miles an hour, catching every single red light. Hollywood hasn't had a single rush hour in decades. If you need to get somewhere in a hurry, you'd better do it between three a.m. and four-thirty a.m.

I pulled to the back of the Hollywood Lingerie Club and joined the drummers of two other bands and a couple guitar players. No one from Dave's band was there yet. We drummers hauled our gear out and set drum kits all the way up right there on the alley's pavement.

This is how it's done in Los Angeles: One band exits and the next one squeezes into the narrow dim-lit hall, up back steps to the stage. If the drummer waits to set up his kit on stage it could cost two, possibly three, songs of time. Clubs all over L.A. operate this way. Jam the bands in and hope they bring a lot of thirsty fans.

Alex the keyboard player was the first to show up.

"Wha's up, Lou?"

We fist bumped. "I'm ready to rock."

"Me too. Got all new chords and batteries. No way am I coming off like a chump this time."

"Aw, it wasn't as bad as all that," I lied. Toward the end of the last show Alex's keyboard kept cutting in and out. He nearly had a meltdown on stage.

"Bullshit it wasn't. Fuckin' ready tonight though, fuckin' A!" Chaney, the bass player, arrived next. Fist bumps went around.

"How's it going Chaney?" I asked.

"Fuckin' landlord's threatening to kick me out."

"That sucks," Alex said. "What's the problem?"

"Noise, supposedly. My music is no louder than the girl above me, it's just that she's hot and my landlord wants to fuck her."

"Why don't you fuck your landlord then," Alex said, thinking he was funny.

"I would, she's hot, but she's a dyke."

Sonny showed up next and chilled me out. If he suspected me of stealing his processor, he didn't show it. I was watching my back just the same.

"I hear Van Halen's going out again, you guys going?" Chaney asked.

"Nah," Alex said. "David Lee Roth can't sing anymore."

"It's Halen dude," Chaney said.

"That's true," I added attempting to fit in—and move the conversation. "I met the drummer who toured with Roth on his later solo stuff. Cat named Ray—good dude."

"That's the dude who played with Korn, too, right?" Alex said.

"Same dude," I said. "So where's Dave?"

"Inside already. He likes to get here early and do his deals," Chaney said.

"Deals?"

"Coke."

"Shut up, dude, fuck," Alex scolded.

"Who cares? You don't care do you, Crasher?"

"About blow? It ain't for me but I don't care either way." It was hard not to think about Bobby laid up in his hospital bed.

The door flew open and the punk rock-sounding band before

us piled out. They were fired up from a good show. We congratulated them. Sonny broke rockers' etiquette and squeezed into the hall before the band was fully done. He created a traffic jam that annoyed the other band and they said so.

Sonny ignored them and pushed his gear through. Chaney apologized to the other band, which cooled the situation.

"He always fucking does that," Alex said, shaking his head.

I hit the stage running and put my bass drum down in the exact right place. I'd barely turned my back when the soundman, or rather, *soundwoman* quickly knelt down and put a mic into the bass drum. Placement was key. If a drummer moves gear after mics are set, sound people snap.

She clipped mics to my toms. Half her head was shaved. The other half was high and spiked down the middle then flowed into short closed-cropped fuzz. She had several earrings, including a nose ring, which suited her. She barely acknowledged me when I introduced myself. I didn't take it personally, she's got a job to do and a short time to do it in.

Abbott stepped on stage briefly. We exchanged a quick nod, nothing more. The other guys seemed focused on setup but with something else. The vibe was chilly. I felt more like an outsider than at the first gig. I wasn't being sensitive. A sideman can't afford to be. No, something was up. I had to play it as though everything was cool and maintain a poker-player's calm.

It was made easy once I glanced at the crowd gathered at the front of the stage. Anytime eye contact was made I was given smiles and thumbs up. I even recognized a few faces from my first gig. This was the intoxicating part. The body fills with positive ions of adrenalin. My professional side kicked in. I was going to nail this show, regardless of my despising Dave Abbott. Besides, some of the best music in history comes from tension and bandmates' mutual hatred for one another.

There was no love lost between the Davies brothers of the Kinks, and they cranked out hit after hit. Apparently the Van Halen brothers and frontman David Lee Roth put out their best tunes while they couldn't stand each other. And if one wants to talk tension, James Brown was known for fining his players per mistake, as well as violent outbursts—yet they pumped out the best funk music of all time.

From the first count in I made the stage my own. I not only drove the band, I had the crowd in the palm of my hand. I made bodies move and hands clap. The sound girl did such a great job that I could literally feel the boom of my bass drum ravage the chest cavities of the patrons. I tagged big endings to the ends of songs, twirled sticks, rose to my feet after a few numbers, and cupped a hand to my ear, commanding the audience to give us more. I received nods and grins from the band. They were turning—Dave excepted, of course.

Three quarters of the way into the set, the crowd called for a drum solo. Those at the front pounded on the stage while others stomped feet. I had two loosely written solos chambered but wouldn't release either without Dave's permission—simple hired-gun etiquette. In the second to last song the band was scheduled to break down the music while Sonny did a slow melodic guitar solo. Before he began he walked over to my drum set.

"When I'm done, I'm gonna vamp the groove and you solo over the top. You cool with that?"

"Thought you'd never ask."

My heartbeat went up. From the moment I learned the song, I felt the repetitive groove near the tune's end screamed for a drum solo. Now I had permission to blow. Still, I didn't have Abbott's go-ahead. To hell with it, Dave was the general but Sonny was my superior officer in this rock 'n' roll platoon.

Sonny moved to center stage. As a tight-knit rhythm section we held the foundation down at a low volume. As Sonny built, we built. We held the tempo but brought the volume up far better than any D.J. could with a volume button. Sonny moved off the slow melodious notes and began rip-rapid notes high up on the axe's fret board. We held tempo but added a few notes of our own. Alex tossed in quick keyboard runs, careful not to step on

Sonny's notes. Instead, they complemented, and at times harmonized, with his notes. The two of them reminded me of old Deep Purple records with guitar player Ritchie Blackmore and keyboard player John Lord.

Chaney began adding percussive notes on his bass, which came off with a fat slapping sound. With my added drum fills we were all cooking with gas. Sonny shredded his way over to Chaney and shouted in his ear, but from the floor it looked like a whisper. He was cluing Chaney in on my upcoming solo. Chaney turned and gave me a big smile. Abbott had the professional sense of standing off-stage left.

The drummer from the previous band stood beside two groupies who were swooning over Sonny. The drummer ignored them, folded his arms and locked eyes on me. He knew what was coming and wanted a look-see. Abbott moved toward the groupies but slowed his stride when he heard Sonny and the guys bring the volume down and loop the heavy line. To his credit he was quick on the uptake. He beelined to the mic at center stage.

"Ladies, gentlemen and assholes, put your hands together for our latest kickass addition on drums—Lou 'the thrasher' Crasher. Rip their faces off, Lou!"

I began with a simple pattern in my feet, which got the crowd clapping as a unit. On top, I went through a series of marching drum rudiments. This took the groove in a military direction that was counter to the song's groove but almost made it funky. Chaney nodded right away. After thirty seconds of this, I upped the tempo and moved up and down between the snare drum and cymbals, accenting the crashes with big bass drum hits. I double-timed my speed. This is easier than it looks and almost always gets whistles from the crowd.

The flashy visual jazz handled, I moved over to my deepest-pitched toms and put a straight-ahead double bass run underneath at around one hundred and thirty beats per minute. At this point, the audience might believe a thunderstorm was happening inside the club. With a good sound system, which the club had, the rumble would shake up more than a few heartbeats and throw off a pacemaker or two. Alex started laughing. As loud as I played, I could hear the crowd going berserk. They'd asked for a solo, and dang, if I wasn't giving them one. For a drummer, there are few better feelings than this on the planet.

Time to big crescendo the hell out of this thing. I began playing fast groups of three, known as triplets, and moved them all over the kit. If anyone in the crowd listened to early solos by Led Zeppelin drummer John Bonham, they'd appreciate my tribute. The thunderstorm suddenly became a category-five hurricane and the audience mopped it up. I picked the drums I wanted and repeated it over and over, giving it a skipping vinyl record sound. I held this for twenty seconds before opening my eyes and getting the band's attention. Sonny raised his axe neck high in the air. When he brought it down, he and the guys hit a big sustained chord. I washed all over the cymbals with rapid double bass underneath. Ten seconds later, we all stopped on a rock 'n' roll dime. The place went wild. Abbott reemerged.

"Lou Crasher, everybody. Does he kick ass or what?"

I grinned ear to ear as my chest heaved up and down. I stood and gave a corny bow as thanks for the support. Chaney and Sonny came back and fist-bumped me. Alex called me an animal from behind his keyboard rig.

"Alex on keys, Sonny on gee-tar, Chaney on the five-string bass, y'all know the Crasher. We had one more for you fucks, but we ain't topping that. I'm Dave, we're Boning Joanie and we're out."

He dropped the mic and walked off stage. I had to admit, it was the right move. I also had to admit Dave Abbott was a good frontman. Shame; I'd still have to burn him down.

I was given heaps of praise as I tore down my kit. The first compliment came from the sound girl.

"Inspiring," she said, and pulled me into a half hug.

"Likewise. I could feel that bass drum from my toes to my nose."

I also received three shots and two beers. I thanked those who needed thanking and downed two of the shots. I left the third, seeing as it was florescent blue in color. I don't drink blue drinks. I put drums into cases and sipped beers in between. The band members' excitement over the solo subsided quickly, as if a thick rain cloud had passed overhead. I acted as if I didn't notice, and loaded and locked everything in my ride.

After one more quick "idiot" check of the stage, I headed to the bathroom. I was washing my hands as Alex, the keyboard player, bolted in.

"There you are."

"What's up? Good show tonight."

"It was nice playin' with ya."

"That sounds like an ending. Your regular guy back?"

"No, just...are ya packed up?"

"Yeah."

He stepped close to whisper, "Fire up your car and get the fuck outta here man."

"Why? What's—"

"Just go. And you didn't hear shit from me."

He stepped nervously out the door. I moved through the crowd like a cat in a dog pen. I searched for Abbott, or any bouncer who looked like they might be on his payroll, but found no one. I tried not to be too stand-offish with all of the congratulators and new fans, but my focus was on saving my hide. Alex had freaked me out.

I opened the door to the alley with caution. An object came at me, eyeball height, with speed. I ducked. A baseball bat slammed into the door. A glimpse says two thousand words. I recognized the batter. I rushed him before he could reload and grabbed him one-handed by the throat, the other on the bat.

"Travis, you little shit," I said, slamming him hard into the side of the building. "I'm gonna—"

I then heard a booming sound and immediately saw a flash. It was just how actor Stacy Keach narrated it all those years ago

173

as Mike Hammer, during a Thursday night episode. A whistle sound was followed by a thunder crack, leading into a flash of light, ending with a snooze. Jake always told me to watch my six, and I hadn't—another fine mess.

I had a head that pounded like a tympani drum and rubber bands for legs. I was held under both arms with legs dragging behind me. Through the haze I could see shapes: people working at tables. I blinked my eyes. The people worked at sectioning out cocaine and putting it into little baggies or counting out stacks of cash.

In front of the two people that dragged me was a big man with a huge back. At the end of a chain leash was a heavy Rottweiler with thick bowed hind legs. The tables ended. I attempted a few steps, hoping my legs would wake up, because if they did, I was taking flight, and soon.

After sixteen more feet of tables, workers were hunched over musical gear, and lots of it. There was even a guy operating a forklift. I recognized every brand of amplifier, drum, guitar, bass and keyboard. This place was Dave Abbott's all the way.

We arrived at an office door. The big man with the dog knocked.

"It's us," he called.

"Bring him in." It was Abbott's voice.

The guys working my arms had trouble getting the three of us through the door. It had a Keystone Cops vibe to it. They lost their grip. I did a slow fall to my knees. They helped me up. We stood in front of a large wooden desk with a fake marble surface. Abbott sat behind it with his fingers interlaced behind his head. With his feet on the desk he looked more cocksure than the morning rooster.

"You treat all your drummers this way?"

"Only the ones that fuck with me, and that's exactly what you did." He unclasped his hands and sat forward. "I gotta take you off the stage—permanently."

I didn't bother waiting for any further dime-store dialogue

and went straight for the element of surprise. I threw a right back elbow to the guard on my right and caught him on the side of the head. It wasn't clean but bought me a moment in time. I threw a left-handed karate chop-style blow to the other guard's throat. He blocked it easily but wasn't ready for my follow-up attack. I squatted low and gave him a solid hook to the groin. He doubled over, hit his head on the desk and went out.

Guard number one, now recovered, came for me but I was already on top of Abbott's desk. Out of the corner of my eye I could see the big man readying to set the Rottweiler off-leash. That would end everything. Abbott tried to slide his chair back but must have caught a wheel on a divot in the cheap linoleum. It was the break I needed.

I landed on top of him and took him and the chair to the ground. I raised my fists. He covered his head with both arms, so I sank a heavy shot into his mid-section. He dropped his hands with an 'oomph,' allowing me to drop a left cross to his eye. It puffed up immediately. As I loaded up for another shot, guard number one got to me and pulled me off.

I was never so delusional that I thought I could take on all of these guys, but I own a strong belief in going down fighting. The guard pulled me backward by my arms. I attempted a back head-butt, but he was out of range. He must not have noticed guard number two, who still slumbered, because he tripped over him while taking us both to the floor. I tried for another back head-butt and caught partial chin this time. As I was gaining my feet, Travis showed up out of nowhere and kicked me hard in the ribs. As he wound up for a second kick, I got to one knee and punched him square in the kneecap.

He went down with a scream. I'd heard that scream before and was beginning to like it. I crawled toward Travis, who did an awkward back crabwalk. Fear filled his coward's eyes. The dog's chain rattled behind me. His growl sounded inches from my neck. I kept crawling. Maybe I could kill Travis before the dog killed me—doubtful but worth a try.

I was almost to the little runt when Dave's calm voice was in my ear.

"Playtime's over, Crasher. You're done."

It was the second time in my life a gun muzzle had been held at my temple. The first time was when my unhinged Uncle Curtis tried to scare me. The big man brought the Rottweiler within inches of my face. I could feel the heat of his breath as he growled low in his chest. Abbott spun the gun around and sapped me with it. I flinched at just the right time, so I didn't go all the way out.

I could barely hear Abbott giving his goons a tongue-lashing for allowing me to get to him. Another voice came into the room. It was vaguely familiar. I struggled to open my eyes. My ears did not deceive me after all. Angela. I tried to speak but nothing came. I couldn't make out the expression on her face. Sadness? Disbelief? Pity perhaps. Travis shoved her aside, then stomped me back to sleep.

CHAPTER 21

Jake sat in his truck at the opposite end of the alley that led to the warehouse. He knew Lou was inside because he'd followed the big truck with the dual back tires from West Hollywood to downtown. Jake ground his teeth and mulled over the facts: Back when Abbott had offered Lou another gig, he'd smelled a rat. Abbott was no dummy, and the gesture signaled that he had plans for Lou. Jake now knew what those plans were.

As he watched the lone sentry, he considered the options. Lou had been inside too long, so Jake was going to have to make a move—soon. A straight-up storming of the gate was his least favorite option, but still an option just the same. A plan took shape. The sentry was the key.

The man didn't hear Jake approach, even though Jake made no effort to conceal himself. *Useless*, Jake thought. That was good.

"Hold it," the sentry said, pointing the business end of a Mossberg pump shotgun with a pistol grip at Jake's chest. It was a weapon good for blasting things apart up close or for law enforcement to blow hinges off doors, but inappropriate for securing a warehouse. As Jake supposed earlier—useless sentry. Jake raised his hands part way and slowed but didn't altogether stop. He wanted to get close and keep the man talking.

"I said hold it there, bud."

"Sorry. I'm looking for Tony's Bar. A waitress I met said to come around back."

"This ain't no bar; now move along."

"That's a shame," Jake said, inching forward. "Well can I use your bathroom real quick?"

"You've got three seconds before this Mossy cuts you in half."

"Three," Jake said but not as a question.

"Yes, three."

"Two."

"What? Are you nuts?"

Jake leapt forward and easily knocked to gun aside with his left forearm and followed it with a stiff right to the sentry's jaw. He caught the man before he fell and shoved him against the wall.

"One," Jake said to the sleeping man as he went through his pockets and dug out a cell phone. He scrolled through the man's contacts until he found Dave Abbott's number. Jake had kept the dialog going with the sentry long enough to carefully study his voice. Mimicry would not be a problem. The man's voice was low and gruff like Jake's. He just needed to make sure he kept it short.

He punched the number in. Dave answered, irritated. Jake was willing to bet Lou was the cause of that irritation.

"Roc, what the fuck do you want?"

"Five-O, five-O tons of them!"

"What? Here?"

"Feds, too…setting up down the alley. I'm out."

"Out my ass, get in here and help pack, you know the EVAC protocol we've—practiced this."

"I'm out." Jake clicked off.

The sentry began moaning. It would still be a while before he came all the way conscious. Jake quickly and thoroughly went through the man's pockets and cleared his weapons. In addition to the Mossberg he had two knives, a switchblade with a short blade, and a Bowie with a five-inch blade and serrated edge on top. Jake shook his head in disgust at the man's sidearm: It was a gold-plated forty-five with a custom bone handle grip with the words "Big Daddy" etched down one side of the barrel.

"Pretender," Jake said, delivering a solid left, this time putting the sentry back to sleep. He put him over his shoulder in a fireman carry over to a dumpster, popped the lid, and dumped him inside. He then crouched beside the dumpster, out of view, and waited. Three full minutes went by before Abbott, the Travis punk, a stocky Latino and a woman fitting Angela's description sprinted past. At the end of the alley they hopped into the dually and sped off. Jake waited another minute. A big group of people, men and women, sprinted down the alley in the opposite direction from Abbott's crew. In the middle of the pack was a big man with a Rottweiler. If an actual raid had been taking place, everyone would have been popped. They took way too long to evacuate.

"Amateurs," Jake said walking to the entrance. He worried what shape Lou would be in.

CHAPTER 22

The world came back into soft focus. I was in a small rectangular-shaped room. I recognized the door, it was off the office. I had no idea how much time had elapsed. My hands were tied tightly behind my back. I wriggled my fingers and attempted to roll my wrists around. I was tied to a wooden chair, but my legs were free—strange. Maybe my captors had been in a hurry.

My wallet and keys were still in my pockets, no cell phone. The door opened slowly, someone's cheap idea of suspense. In limped Travis with a dumb grin on his face.

"So the little shit-bird is awake." He came in and closed the door behind him.

"I see you've forgotten the message I sent you, Travis."

"Not at all, but ya see, I got a crew and you've just got one asshole."

"Crew, Travis? More like a Taylor Swift squad."

He edged closer. "You're gonna die, Travis," I said.

"Not before you, I'm not."

He came in for a shot but stopped short noticing my legs were untied. Tough luck for me because I was passionately ready to kick him three months into the future.

"How long have you been with Abbott?"

"Two years, and already my crew's—"

"Squad."

"Crew, asshole. Operates on its own, totally independently. Pretty soon it's gonna be *my* name people will know. Too bad you won't be around to see it."

"Never going to happen, Travis. You're not smart enough to run a crew and Dave's not giving up the reins, so you'll just have to be the punk that settles for the scraps from Dave's coke table."

His eyes went wide. He came close again and stopped.

"But wait, I'm gonna take Dave out of the game so that would leave you. And then well, I'll kill you, make it look like you died watching cheap porn."

Travis laughed. My ribbing didn't take.

"I know you, Crasher. You're a shitty drummer, a sad attempt at a Boy Scout and you'll never get what you're after."

"Keep talking, little man."

The smile kept up. "You're just lucky it wasn't me driving that night at your dumbass workplace. I wanted to drive right over your crappy beater, but my boy was too much of a pussy."

"I told you it was a Taylor Swift squad," I shifted in my seat to try and combat numbness.

"So you hit my place, huh?"

His bony chin jutted out in a prideful smile.

"Hate to break it to ya, champ, but I recovered everything your *squad* stole."

"Stop calling it that!" he shouted. His little chest moved up and down until the annoying grin returned.

"Say brutha, any trouble getting the gear back to the rightful owner?"

Whatever my face revealed made him laugh. I suddenly remembered the image of Angela standing over me. I suppose it wasn't a dream after all. Travis walked back out of the room laughing.

As I moved my eyes over the surroundings, searching for weapons and escape routes, I went over Travis's words. He knew something, like an inside joke that wasn't funny. I was just putting it all together when Travis, Abbott and the guard with the Rottweiler came in. The smirk still played on Travis's face. My only satisfaction was that I'd caused his limp with my prior kneecap shot.

Abbott came close but not within kicking distance. I wanted to mock his black eye but refrained. The big man and dog stood behind him. I was glad the dog had no interest in me; that was until he gave it the command of "focus." Then the dog tugged at the leash and put his brownish-yellow eyes on me.

"Travis," Abbott said, "you forgot to tie his legs."

"Not my fault boss—"

"What did I say about excuses?" he shouted. "Tie him up right."

Travis grabbed rope off the wall and approached like a mouse to cheese in a trap. I shuffled my feet quickly, feigning a kick. He jumped backward.

"A real tough guy," I said.

The big man brought the dog closer to me. The dog's lips curled in a snarl. I was ready to comply with my legs being tied. Once bound, Abbott and Travis worked me over pretty good. They gave crosses to the face and gut shots. I tried to use mind over matter like a yogi focuses on her breathing. At some point the door flew open. Even though I was close to passing out, my mind and vision were clear as bells when I saw Angela burst in.

"Stay back, Ang'," Dave said. "He fucked with my business, now he *gets* fucked."

"Angela," I slurred through bloody teeth.

Angela pushed through like she was going to hug me and stopped. She folded her arms and grinned in near slow motion. Her grin turned to mocking laughter.

"Oh Louis, you're such an easy mark."

The guys joined in the laughter.

"Can you guys believe this drummer thought he could play P.I.?" she said, making air quotation marks around "P.I." More laughter. She brought her face an inch from mine.

"Dave is right. You fucked with his, *our* business, and well, here we are."

"Congratulations, Angela. You just made it to my list, right under Travis in fact," I said.

"Thinks he's a tough guy," she said, garnering more laughter. She came in close again and this time wrapped her arms around my neck. I flinched. She slid one hand down my back, slipped something solid in my hand, then kissed me gently on the cheek.

"It's a shame, the sex was actually good."

She let out a final sharp laugh and walked out of the room.

Abbott's cell rang. He checked the screen and answered in a pissed-off tone, then went out the door. The others followed. Angela never looked back.

I fumbled the object around in my hands. It was a knife. I turned it around until I worked the blade out, cutting myself slightly in the process. My hands were tied at the wrist, which caused me to flip the knife butt-side down and saw north-south. I worked feverishly.

Getting through three dudes and a Rottweiler with a knife was a longshot, but I'd take any shot if only to kill Travis. My vision was blurred in my left eye—must have been swelling up. The blade was sharp. I sawed away. One inch up and one inch down. Little strands of fiber popped until the rope gave. My hands were free. I quickly cut my legs out of bondage. I stood, massaged my wrists and did a couple of quick knee bends. In the corner was a raggedy old mop. The handle snapped over my knee. With the knife secure in my back pocket, and mop handle in hand, I crept to the door and put my ear to it.

Several voices were on the other side. They sounded panicked. It also sounded like movers were pushing furniture around the room. Abbott's voice was the loudest. They were pulling up stakes, had to be. Although if they were cleaning house and about to fly the coop, then I'd be a surviving witness—a loose end. I was in a bad spot. Knowing Abbott, he'd probably send the big man with the dog to finish me off. I calculated that he'd open the door and let the dog enter first. I needed the dog deep into the room, leaving me a shot at the big man. I could stab him in the side of the neck, shove him into the room, and haul ass. But I could easily miss my mark with him being on high alert.

I'd go with the mop handle instead. I stood to the side of the door, holding the weapon in both hands; one hand in an underhand grip, the other over with hands about eighteen inches apart. With knees slightly bent, I held the mop handle at shoulder height. When he or anyone other than Angela entered I'd give them a double stab motion to the temple. It would be enough to stun the big man, so I could slide behind him and shove him into the room. Timing would be everything, and as a drummer, timing is my bag.

The doorknob turned slowly. I attempted to slow my breathing and relax my muscles so they wouldn't cramp. But I had more tension than Steinway piano wire. The doorknob stopped its rotation. Then, after a half measure of music, it returned to its original position.

Through the door I heard the big man utter the best phrase I could have hoped for. "Fuck this," he said. Then I heard footsteps and the dog-chain jingle fade in volume away from the door. I listened a little longer before trying the knob. It was unlocked. I peeked into the office. The lingering smell of people remained but they were gone. I moved forward like a soldier negotiating a minefield.

I slid into the warehouse silently. A woman in bra and panties sprinted toward the door. She carried a black bag. Cash spilled out as her little feet bounced across the floor. The gig was up and she was taking a little travel money—good for her. I decided to poke around until the cavalry showed up, which I was certain was on its way. It would have been nice to walk out and find Abbott in handcuffs, being hauled away, but he was free—for the moment.

I thought back to Spivey. He had a drug dealer with the letter D in his phone. I stood in a warehouse where a miscreant moved cocaine and musical equipment. Spivey easily could have told Abbott about the drum, not knowing who Dave actually was. I wanted Spivey's snare drum to be here so bad it hurt. I had to at least do a search—battered as I was, I was still on the job.

The coke seemed to have been removed. I didn't care about that until I thought of Bobby.

"Shit," I whispered out loud.

Hopefully there'd be enough particles for the CSI crew to link the bad coke to Abbott. I walked to the stacks of equipment. Looking at the dust on the floor revealed that some pieces had been taken. When I saw the quality and quantity of gear my blood began to boil. The stacks were easily fourteen-feet high.

Abbott, or someone on his payroll had organized the gear according to instrument and brand better than any music store I'd been in. The drums were at the far end of the stacks, neatly organized, with the snare drums at the top of the heap. I walked back toward the office and found an extension ladder. I stretched it out and leaned it against the cases as I climbed near the top step.

Half the snares were in cases, the others out in the open, sitting sideways on makeshift shelving. None of the exposed snares were Spivey's but there were some beauts for sure. Too many drummers were without their gear. I looked at a stack of cases next and found my mark immediately. One case stood out. It was like a flight case only the metal straps were brushed copper and the rivets appeared to be gold. The case was thicker by about two and a half inches than the other cases. Whatever was inside had value, was precious. I couldn't reach it from my perch so I climbed back down and moved the ladder over. I brought the case down and stared at her a moment.

"Here goes nothing," I said, listening to my voice bounce around the empty warehouse. Two metal latches pulled out on smooth springs and flexed into wing nuts. I twisted them clockwise until the latches made a "pop" sound. The lid was well oiled—she rose silently. The drum was pure handmade beauty. I was reminded of the characters in the movie *The Red Violin*; their faces told a thousand stories when they heard it played. My thoughts travelled all the way back to the fields this country was forged on. What notes were played moving troops left or right? What did the drummer play when he wanted a platoon to charge a hill or fall back? What did Frederick Douglass do with this magnificent creation? Did he play? Or did he put it under glass?

Bobby, Spivey, Angela, the Carruthers family—everyone— flashed through my mind in snapshots, tiny snapshots as if they were all so much smaller than this instrument. I hadn't expected to be hit so hard. I got down on one knee and took her out as if she were a priceless work of art. She slid easily out of the plush velvet interior of the case. She was heavy. My guess was solid oak, older than I'll ever be. She had thick hoops with five lugs that held the skin over the drum's surface and snare side.

The natural wood was honey-nut brown—still round, still smooth after all she'd seen and sang. She may have sung on the wrong side battle but it wasn't her fault. She was crafted, owned and played, and later retired to the hands of a great man.

"Will you ever play her?" The voice came from behind me. I quickly but gently put the drum back in the case, spun around and dug for the knife in my back pocket. I relaxed when I saw Jake standing totem-pole still.

"Come look at her," I said, after what felt like five minutes of gathering my ability to speak. Jake approached and gazed down at her in silence. I gave him a spirited abridged version of her history and my minor part in it all. Still, he stood in silence. I could see his jaw muscles contracting. He was as moved as I was, that much was obvious.

I cleared my throat. "Abbott and his staff skinned out. Something spooked them—like cops were going to raid the place or a bigger player was making a move. While I'm still an amateur P.I., can I assume you had a hand in it all?"

He looked at me and said nothing before putting his eyes

back to the drum.

"Well, thanks," I said. "As to your question, no I'll never play her, she's too..." my mind searched for the right word, "...precious."

"Fair enough. Pack it up and let's go."

CHAPTER 23

The warehouse wasn't far from Jake's loft. Other than the rumble from the Hemi engine we rode in silence. I'd never been to his place before. It was exactly what I'd expect from Jake. It was huge, as lofts tend to be. One side had floor-to-ceiling windows, which put them at sixteen feet in height. His kitchen had a ten-foot concrete countertop island with pots hanging over the white farmhouse sink. Six chunky wood stools sat at the island.

His appliances were all stainless steel and top of the line. The kitchen floor and surrounding area was a dark walnut that flowed into a cement floor that he'd applied a high-gloss clear coat to. Beside the elevator door, off to the left, was a motorcycle built by the Italian company, Ducati, with a flat matte cobalt blue gas tank. Next to this area was a gym. He had ropes, mats, heavy bags, ladders, chin-up bars, a stationary bike, TV screens and more. A large cabinet sat beside a long wall of mirrors. One of the doors was ajar, revealing martial art weapons nunchucks, bow staffs, police batons and scythes.

Massive Yin and Yang symbols were painted on the floor leading away from the gym. The main seating area had a thick odd-shaped piece of driftwood for a coffee table. It must have needed to be craned in—or maybe just loaded onto Jake's back.

I flopped on one of the two large couches that surrounded

the table. Jake pulled a bottle from a cabinet along with two glasses. The bottle turned out to be Johnny Walker Blue scotch. He handed me a glass. We clinked.

"Goes down like salted butter."

"Mm hmm."

"How far back did you pick up my trail? Were you at the gig?"

"Yes."

"And you saw Abbott and his band of merry goons take me?" Jake nodded.

"I didn't watch my six," I said, taking another sip.

"Warned you about that."

"You did."

Silence rolled by, as it does with Jake.

"I saw your girl," he said.

It was my turn to nod.

"It happens," he said.

He came back with water and two pain tablets for me. I took the pills and knocked them back with the Johnny. I left the water.

It was nearly ten a.m. when I woke on his couch.

CHAPTER 24

Jake put together a power shake. It tasted surprisingly good, considering its deep green hue. We decided to go back to the cop shop to try our luck, figuring we had a good shot this time because we had more information. After a short wait we got a confident cop with intelligence behind his eyes. He'd be chief one day, I was sure of it. Finally, somebody took us seriously. He promised to send units to the warehouse, and also to the location we gave for Abbott's trucks.

He moved with added urgency when I mentioned the cocaine might be the tainted coke that'd been plaguing the city. On top of this, he said they put a BOLO on Dave Abbott. Jim Rockford taught this amateur P.I. that BOLO is short for *Be on the Lookout*.

After that, Jake took me back to the Hollywood Lingerie Club. We got out and checked my ride over carefully. The ol' gal had full tire pressure in the tires; the engine appeared tamper-free, and my entire drum set was locked in the car—that part was a miracle. Abbott and his boys must have really been in a hurry, or perhaps there were witnesses. I popped the trunk and made space for Spivey's snare drum.

My gal fired up on the first try. I smiled and rolled the window down.

"She's purring," I said to Jake. "Who knew a journeyman drummer could make enough noise in this town to cause the Serve and Protect boys to put out a BOLO?"

"You're in it now, Lou. Things will come with this," Jake said, and walked back to his ride.

Before I put the ol' gal into drive I remembered to call the hospital and check on Bobby. I checked both pockets before it came back to me that Abbott had taken my phone. My mind bounced back and forth between Bobby and Angela. What was Angela's deal? Sure, she helped me, but why was she hitched to Abbott's wagon? Wishful thinking said that Abbott must have had something on her, she was forced into working with him. Logic told me they were legit business partners. Ouch. In which case she and I were done. Shame.

Even though my body ached, I took the stairs to my place. I was in no mood to bump into a neighbor and chit-chat as to why my face looked like two woodpeckers had attacked me in my sleep. From the end of my hall I could see something on the floor outside my door. Warning bells went off.

On a plain piece of white paper sat my cell phone. The paper had a simple instruction written in crayon:

Call Eddie Carruthers ASAP.

I bolted into my apartment and did a quick sweep. Everything seemed to be in order. I called Eddie.

"Lou?" Eddie's voice was weak. "Stay away, son. Don't come here."

The phone rustled as it was grabbed away. A familiar voice came on the line, vengeful and raspy. It sent a cold shudder through my guts.

Dave Abbott said, "Get your ass over here or I croak these old fucks. And no cops."

The line went dead.

CHAPTER 25

I rolled through three stop signs and blew two red lights. If I got any cop attention I'd bolt and lead them straight to Abbott, even though he said no cops. As I was on my last corner, my phone rang. It was my boss Michael Carruthers.

"Are you kidding me?" I barked to the night air. I didn't want to answer but decided I needed to in case he somehow knew about his parents or was holed up with them.

"Hey Michael, what's up?" I said with exaggerated cheer.

"The guys from Daddy's Porn Stash say they prepaid for today, but you haven't marked it in the book. And they, ah, say they paid a black, an African American."

"It's not in the book because they're lying, boss, and this isn't the first time. Anything else?"

"They're playing the 'customer's always right card.'"

"Tell them to play it somewhere else. Cut 'em loose, boss."

"I wasn't calling for a suggestion, I just wanted to know—"

"Now you know. Gotta go, that's my grandmother on the other line," I lied. "I gotta take this, sorry."

I hung up, feeling bad about not letting Michael in on the danger his parents were in, but I knew him: He'd rush over to the house and get all of us killed.

I lucked out with a parking spot near the door. It was metered but I ignored it. Shutting the ride down, I hefted my steering-wheel club to the building. When the front door opened for a slim Asian man with thick-rimmed glasses, I slipped in behind. A *Wired* magazine peeked out the top of his hemp mini grocery bag.

"Excuse me, do you live here? I don't recognize you."

"Friends on twelfth," I said, hopping into the elevator. Ready to jab the panel, but an out-of-order sign was stuck over the numbers.

"Damn it!"

"I could have told you that was out of order."

"You could have, yeah," I said sprinting past him.

The smart money would say to take the stairs two at a time and jog three-quarter speed to save my energy. But Eddie was in bad shape. I shuddered to think how Evie was holding up. I hit the steps with everything I had. I was puffing by the sixth.

"This ain't nothing like football practice, Crasher, now haul ass!" I shouted. Slowing by the ninth, I put the club in my right hand and began grabbing the handrail with my left hand on the corners. It actually helped.

I nearly bought it crashing through the exit door on the twelfth. I bolted down the narrow hall. If any of the tenants came out at that moment, we'd have a category-five collision.

I pressed my ear to the door. Nothing. I made a decision cops make daily. Hauling my foot back, I kicked the door hard near the bolt. The hollow core door gave easily and smashed the inside wall. Eddie sat in his usual lounger. He was alive but motionless, with a trickle of blood flowing from his temple down to his cheek. His eyes carried a smoky veil of rage.

Evie sat on the couch with her tiny hands clasped on her lap. Tears flowed from her eyes, but she made no sound. She shook slightly and with good reason. Dave Abbott sat beside her with a cheesy grin on his mug and a mean-looking pistol on his lap. Satisfied I'd taken in the scene, he put the muzzle to Evie's temple. She didn't so much as flinch. Tough broad.

Gripping the club tightly, I eased forward.

"Abbott, I'm going to kill you and your five closest friends."

Without taking his eyes off me, he pulled the slide back. It was ready to fire.

"Son," Eddie warned. "Cocking that Taurus automatic was a big mistake."

"Shut up, old man," Dave said.

Travis came out from the bedroom.

"Nothing here worth a shit. Oh hey, Crasher, ready for some fun?"

I moved toward Travis. He raised his hoodie up at the waist, revealing a duplicate gun to Abbott's in his waistband.

"Not so fast, *boy.*"

"Okay, losers, you've got the peacekeepers. What's the play here?"

"My place is crawling with cops. Same with my girl Candy, and that's on you, Crasher."

"I don't care. Un-cock the roscoe, put it on the table, take the little shit-minion and piss off."

"Don't leave that thing within my reach," Evie said. "I'll put three in his spine before he reaches the door."

"Ha, even the broad is a tough guy," Abbott said, turning to me. "You hurt my businesses, Crasher, so I'm going to hurt what you care about."

"Bullshit," I said.

"Agreed," Eddie echoed.

Eddie and Evie's demeanor changed. They were becoming steeled.

"Evie, are you all right?"

"Yes, Eddie, what about that knock on the head?"

"This? Ha! My dead sister hits harder than this punk. God rest her."

"Shut up," Dave shouted. "Everyone just shut up."

"Son, you're all out of moves," Eddie said. "You shoot us, and a dozen witnesses will make you before you hit the lobby."

"And you're not a gunman, Abbott, you're a thief and a drug dealer," I said.

"He said shut it, Crasher," Travis said.

"And when you're caught, how well do you think you'll do with that tiny frame of yours, Travis? Be smart, stay out of jail and run your own crew, that's what you really want anyway.

Abbott caught his breath, moved the gun from Evie to me and fired. I took the bullet where the shoulder meets the bicep, spun and went down. It stung like I'd been prodded with a hot poker.

"Louis!" Eddie shouted.

I landed on my side. Either adrenalin kicked in or I was only winged because the pain was gone. Evie pulled her hand up and back-hand slapped Abbott hard across the face. I struggled to my feet, which caught Abbott's attention and saved Evie from being pistol-whipped.

He lunged forward and came at me with the gun. Travis jumped out of his way and stumbled toward the kitchen. Eddie moved like a man with training and brought his bone-handled cane down hard on Abbott's gun hand. I was on my feet and launched airborne toward Abbott. The gun went off. The bullet tore into the dining room table leg. Abbott and I collided and flew over the arm of the couch. As we pitched to the right, we collided with an antique hutch with glass pane doors. I squeezed my eyes shut as my head broke the glass.

Bouncing off the hutch I landed on top of Abbott. Two rights landed on his face before he overpowered me and rolled us over. I blocked two shots before he got a left through to my eye and dazed me. Still, I managed to deflect two more shots and buck him off by flipping my hips.

I was back on top and dropping bombs but couldn't get past his thick forearms.

"Body, Lou, body," Eddie shouted.

I dropped a heavy right elbow to Abbott's rib cage. I heard a snap sound as his side caved in with the blow. He cried out. I'd broken a floating rib. No time to rejoice as I'd mistakenly rolled him close to the roscoe. He grabbed it, thrust it at my face and fired. I moved just in time. The bullet flew into the ceiling and no doubt up to the neighbor's apartment.

My ears rang. I couldn't believe a guy I'd shared a stage with would try and blast my face apart. We lay side-by-side and wrestled for the gun. Out of the corner of my eye I saw Travis creeping forward with his gun out. I couldn't see where Eddie and Evie were, but this was all but over for me. As Abbott and I rolled back and forth I caught glimpses of Eddie creeping up behind Travis. Travis pointed the gun, trying to get a clear shot at me, but Eddie delivered the mail with his cane once more. Travis's gun flew out of his hand. He turned and lunged for Eddie.

Abbott and I were side-by-side again. One of his fingers found the trigger and squeezed. The gun spoke, my ears rang again. Another sound like a church bell sang out. It wasn't a gunshot this time. Evie got behind Travis and whacked his skull with an old-school cast-iron skillet. Travis dropped like a rock, followed by the skillet a second later. Travis lay not five feet from us. My left index finger slipped inside the trigger guard. I fired. Missed.

My hands were getting sweaty. I was losing my grip. I risked releasing my left hand and jabbed a thumb into Abbott's eye socket. Sank it deep. He screamed and yanked hard. The move caused me to fire again. The gun roared for the sixth time. The top right quadrant of Abbott's skull from cheekbone to hairline blew apart. He stopped moving.

The room smelled of gunpowder, sweat and death. I rolled onto my back and sucked air into my lungs, gulping. I stared at the bullet hole in the ceiling and wondered if the neighbors were all right. Eddie and Evie were talking, but it was muffled under the ringing in my ears.

I rolled back on my side and looked at Travis. Just then Eddie's words became audible.

"Six shots in all. Your two shots put two men down. You're a hell of a shot, Lou Crasher."

I craned my neck to look. The stray bullet had caught Travis on the top of his head. Two men down with partial skulls. I gagged but didn't throw up. Struggling to my feet, I was still on hands and knees when Michael Carruthers ran into the apartment.

"Mom! Dad! What the hell?"

He rushed to his parents. The three of them huddled on the couch. I managed to get to the kitchen and poured myself a big glass of water. Knocked it back. I carefully put the glass down and held onto the sink with both hands. I started to shake. I shook as if an earthquake had run through me from head to toe. Eventually, Evie came and put a gentle arm around my shoulders.

I'd only fired at targets with my uncle. Now I'd killed two men. The body tremors continued. I was still shaking when four cops and two paramedics came through the door. Evie never left my side—never stopped rubbing my back and telling me it was going to be okay.

EPILOGUE

The paramedics did a bang-up job of patching this banged-up P.I. But it wasn't enough to get me through the grueling hours of answering police questions. You can't hold a man for defending himself with lethal force if the situation demands it. I was finally kicked loose, naturally with an order not to leave town. I took an Uber to my ride and drove home ten miles under the speed limit. When I got home my landline was ringing. It was Angela.

"How are you?"

"Tired as hell but happy to be alive."

I could tell she was nervous. "I need to explain a few things."

I gave her silence so she could do her thing.

"I just wanted to say I'm so sorry for all that happened to you. I never meant to hurt you; I really was trying to help you out."

I didn't say anything.

"Are you still there?"

"I'm here."

"Lou, I don't know what else to say. I did hear what happened though, all of it, and I'm so—"

"Angela, you sent me after your gear, knowing who stole it, and now I've got a lawyer I can't afford trying to keep me out of jail. Now, if she keeps me out she can't promise that Homeland

Security won't send me back to the great white north so, if there's nothing else, I gotta grab some sleep before going to visit Bobby—who, by the way—came out of his coma...a medically induced coma, courtesy of the cocaine you and Abbott—" I trailed off. "You know what? I'm done."

"Wait," she was crying, "I'm not part of that."

"Oh? You're just in on the gear-theft angle? I thought you were a musician."

"I am, it was meant to be temporary. I just needed some quick cash. You of all people should know how much it costs to run a band. Not to mention all of the crap I have to put up with being a woman in this business."

"People died. People went into comas and you, temporary or not, and directly or otherwise with the coke, were in business with that bastard."

She sobbed into the phone. "I screwed up, okay? I admit my ambition got in the way. It's not the first time, but I'm working on it. Please don't cash us out, we have something good."

"I'm sorry, doll, but my closest acquaintance nearly bought it. How am I supposed to get past that?"

She sobbed some more. I could hear her sniffle and try to pull herself together.

"So you don't want me. You're not willing to forgive me but answer me one question at least. Did the cops...did they, did my name come up at all?"

"Wow, you are good. The tears, the apology...that must have been the potatoes and now here's the real meat of the conversation. Are the cops looking at partners and associates of the guy that put people in the hospital and stole countless thousands of dollars' worth of gear? Hmm, I don't recall if your name came up, but I can't promise it won't. And if they ask, who knows how it'll play out?"

"I really did call to say sorry. I was just wondering—"

"It was nice rockin' n rollin' with ya, doll, but honestly, you scare the hell out of me."

"Then I guess this is good—"

"So long, doll."

My cell buzzed immediately after her call. I was in no mood, and was about to let it ring, when I saw it was Eddie Carruthers.

"Eddie, how are you two holding up?"

"I'm calling to ask you that. You were the one got shot."

"I'm good. Just grazed, after all. You might find the bullet in a cabinet somewhere."

"And the cops? They were nice enough to question us here but I'm sure they grilled you at the station once the paramedics cleared you."

"That they did. I'm going to be fine, don't you two worry. How's Michael, is he upset that I didn't clue him into what was happening?"

"At first, but we steered him in the right direction. Remember how he was acting kinda screwy? Showing up late, going AWOL and so on?"

"Certainly do."

"Well I've been dyin' to tell you what he's been up to. The knucklehead got it into his brain that he and I weren't bonding enough; something we didn't do in my day, by the way. Anyway, he goes to one of them adult schools and signs up for football sciences."

"Football sciences? You mean a course that teaches you the game of football?"

"You got it. He's been going three nights a week and studying like a maniac." Eddie paused. I could hear his voice get caught in his throat. "All so he could watch football with his dear old dad. Ain't that the darndest thing?"

"It's kind of sweet, Big Eddie. Think I'll stay home for the next couple Sundays, give you two a chance to get to know each other."

"That might not be a bad idea. But you better get your butt over here for playoffs. Football sciences or not, he's just gonna have to accept that Lou Crasher's part of this family...at least during football season." He chuckled.

Three days went by. My body was bruised and my heart was broken. The bruises healed on their own. I pieced my heart back together with drums, sandwiches and scotch. On day four a knock came on my door. Jake.

He stood in boots, jeans, black tee, leather jacket and helmet under one arm. When his quick survey of me was complete, he walked past.

"What's happening Jake?"

"How did it go with the cops?"

"It should be cool. The trucks were moved but the cops located them a couple miles east of the Budweiser plant. They also got trace elements of coke at the warehouse. Abbott was cutting the blow with laundry detergent."

"Dealers have been doing that for years; hasn't caused people to drop like flies."

"Ah, but Abbott was using a product made in China, sold only in Mexico. The detergent isn't even sold in China anymore. They've banned it. Obviously there's still product floating around out there and Abbott's been using it—*was* using it."

"He brought it in from Mexico?"

"So I'm told. I can't imagine he'd save much cash per ounce of coke but what do I know?"

My cell phone rang. It was Rex Spivey. I told Jake I needed to take it. Rex's voice was calmer than before. Maybe it was a note of respect.

"I've seen the news but thought I'd give you a day or two to chill out."

"Appreciate it. I'm chilled."

"I nearly choked on my meal when I saw my dealer on the news. Dave Abbott! They popped him for the gear ring, as well as the cocaine, right? Oh my god, right?"

"He was a bad man, Rex. You're lucky to be alive, running

his poison into you."

"True, true, so don't keep a good man in suspense. Did he have my drum? Did the son of a bitch rob me?"

"He certainly did."

"I knew you were on to something the minute you asked to see my phone. When ya bringing her by?"

"When I found her, I told a buddy of mine I'd never play her."

"Right, no way. Too precious."

"But then I really looked her over. So I grabbed my jazz sticks, the light seven-A's, barely heavier than chop sticks."

"Oh no."

"Rex, I played the gentlest buzz roll on her. She sang like a peaceful hive of honey bees. And that was it."

"You never should have played her, Lou."

"I know."

"I'm not getting her back, am I?"

"She needs to be shared. Children on field trips need to see her, to know her history. Tourists from the world over must experience her beauty."

"Where is she?"

"The National Museum of American History."

"That's what I get for hiring a drummer P.I. to find a snare drum, I guess." He laughed.

"Should have hired a guitar player."

"Guitar player would have given up after ten minutes."

"True. Sorry, Rex."

"Don't be, I've got plenty of dough and I'll make more. Sad you won't see any of that money I promised you."

"Been crying about it all morning."

"You're a good dude, Crasher. I'll send you a check for expenses anyway. I'm not a total dick."

"Thanks. I feel like crap though. It's not like me to leave a song unplayed through to the end."

"I'm glad you feel shitty but in reality you did the right thing, ya fucking Boy Scout." He laughed again.

"Say, I'm having a real shitkicker of a party tonight. I'm talking peyote, strippers and a real native Indian sweat lodge. Are you in?"

"Did exactly that just last night. Thanks anyway."

"Yeah right, ya big liar. You take care."

"Will do."

I put the phone on my tiny kitchen table. Jake nodded. I could tell he approved of the conversation. I talked him into one of my turkey club sandwiches. Dialogue was light as we worked through them. My fridge held quality pilsner, IPA, Japanese beer and Boston lager. It turned out the Japanese was the best pairing with the Crasher club sandwich.

At one point Jake spilled some crumbs on his jeans. He did a little pat, pat, brush technique on the denim that was oddly familiar to me.

"How are you with the shootings?" he asked.

"Meaning?"

"I'm assuming you never killed a man before. Now you killed two."

"I'm holding up all right. It was justified."

"That helps," he nodded and pulled a business card out of his wallet and slid it across the table. It contained a woman's name and phone number. No title or company name.

"Who's this?"

"A friend. She's a psychotherapist. A good one. No shame in talking to someone. A feeling comes with killing a man."

"Two," I said.

I stared at the card before putting into my pocket, unsure if I'd call. I recycled our empties, grabbed two more beers and sat back down.

This was the most dialogue we'd had since I'd known Jake, so I kept it going.

"Okay Jake, cards on the table. I helped you out ages ago on the store robbery, yet you've paid me back ten times over. Why?"

"Cards on the table?"

"Yes," I said. "All fifty-two of them."

"Your parents met at the University of Toronto."

"What? How did—"

"They met, dated, graduated, got married, then had you."

"Uh huh."

"What you didn't know is that during the courtship they took a break, about eight months. Your dad met a woman named Coretta Strickland. They had a son. Coretta kept it from your dad until her child was about two years old. By this time your parents were married.

Your dad sent money, but Coretta always sent it back. She was proud. After months of trying, your dad stopped sending checks. He spoke to the kid a few times into his teens then tapered it off. As far as I know, your mother doesn't know about any of this."

"I need something stronger than this," I said, grabbing a bottle of ten-year scotch from under my sink. Jake refused. I took a two-finger blast.

"Assuming all of this is true, how'd you know about all of this...or have any interest in this?"

"I'm Jake Strickland. Coretta's son. We're half-brothers."

I started to pour another shot and stopped. We stared at each other. I started to laugh. My laughter grew almost to the point of hysterical.

"How is this funny?" he asked.

"I've been hangin' with you for nearly two years and never figured out who you were. Some..." I laughed harder "...some P.I. I turned out to be." I kept laughing. I grabbed another glass and poured two scotches. He didn't decline.

"To brothers, rock n roll, and a job well done," I wheezed.

We clinked, drank and put the tumblers down.

"Now that we're family and all, exactly what line of work are you in, Jake?"

ACKNOWLEDGMENTS

Right off the top I need to thank my lovely wife Sonia. You steady me when I falter, make me laugh when I'm on the brink of losing it and make me smile on the daily. Love ya, doll. To my dear departed parents Rosemary and Bill, thank you, thank you, thank you. I miss you deeply. I want to thank my siblings Cleta and Gary because I know you have my six. Ismael Tavera, you're the best police consultant/friend a dude could ever have. I'd like to thank Anne Hillerman, Shawn Reilly Simmons and Paul D. Marks—great friends, great writers. Thanks to William Glavin V for sharing your expertise on firearms. Elaine Ash, thank you for your edits, friendship and steady guidance that led me through the doors of Down & Out Books!

JONATHAN BROWN is the author of *A Boxing Trainer's Journey: A Novel Based of the Life of Angelo Dundee* and the novella *Moose's Law: A Doug "Moose" McCrae Story* about an ex-football-playing bouncer and "fixer" living in Los Angeles. Brown has also written short stories that have appeared in *Out of the Gutter Online* and in two Palos Verdes library anthologies. In addition, he has written, recorded and performed an audio children's book, *KANU: A Boy's Journey*. His second book in the Lou Crasher series drops in 2020 from Down & Out Books. He currently teaches drums and is a personal trainer. He and his wife enjoy sunny-living in Los Angeles.

JonathanBrownWriter.com

BOOKS

On the following pages are a few
more great titles from the
Down & Out Books publishing family.

For a complete list of books and to
sign up for our newsletter,
go to DownAndOutBooks.com.

Skunk Train
Joe Clifford

Down & Out Books
December 2019
978-1-64396-055-5

Starting in the Humboldt wilds and ending on the Skid Row of Los Angeles, *Skunk Train* follows two teenagers, who stumble upon stolen drug money, with drug dealers, dirty cops, and the Mexican mob on their heels.

On a mission to find his father, Kyle heads to San Francisco, where he meets Lizzie Decker, a wealthy high school senior, whose father has just been arrested for embezzlement. Together, Kyle and Lizzie join forces, but are soon pursued by Jimmy, the two dirty cops, and the Mexican cartel, as a third detective closes in, attempting to tie loose threads and solve the Skunk Train murders.

Trouble & Strife
Crime Stories Inspired by Cockney Rhyming Slang
Simon Wood, Editor

Down & Out Books
December 2019
978-1-64396-056-2

Welcome to the world of Cockney rhyming slang, where what is said means something completely different than it sounds. Originally, it was a coded language created by criminals for deceiving undercover police officers during Victorian times. For *Trouble & Strife*, those coded and colorful phrases became the inspiration for eleven killer crime stories.

Edited by Simon Wood with stories by Steve Brewer, Susanna Calkins, Colin Campbell, Angel Luis Colón, Robert Dugoni, Paul Finch, Catriona McPherson, Travis Richardson, Johnny Shaw, Jay Stringer, and Sam Wiebe.

Price Hike
Preston Lang

All Due Respect, an imprint of
Down & Out Books
October 2019
978-1-64396-041-8

Jane is a struggling con artist, estranged from her ex and her sick son.

When she tricks a dangerous criminal out of some black-market meds, it puts her family in danger, and they go on the run, chased by a dark criminal syndicate as well as the CEO of a widely-detested pharma corp.

Price Hike is a fast-paced tale of con games, corporate greed, and one of the douchiest bros of modern times.

Chasing China White
Allan Leverone

Shotgun Honey, an imprint of
Down & Out Books
September 2019
978-1-64396-029-6

When heroin junkie Derek Weaver runs up an insurmountable debt with his dealer, he's forced to commit a home invasion to wipe the slate clean.

Things go sideways and Derek soon finds himself a multiple murderer in the middle of a hostage situation.

With seemingly no way out, he may discover the key to redemption lies in facing down long-ignored demons.

Made in the USA
Columbia, SC
22 November 2019